D0422728

Give It Up, Mom

Give It Up, Mom

Mary Robinson

Houghton Mifflin Company
Boston   1989

Library of Congress Cataloging-in-Publication Data

Robinson, Mary, 1939–
   Give it up, Mom / Mary Robinson.
     p. cm.
   Summary: Twelve-year-old Rayne's friendship with Wendy and Dionna
gives her the support she needs as she pursues her school project,
to help her mother quit smoking.
   ISBN 0–395–49700–0
   [1. Smoking—Fiction. 2. Friendship—Fiction.] I. Title.
PZ7.R56752Gi 1989   89–1767
[Fic]—dc19   CIP
                 AC

Printed in the United States of America

P 10 9 8 7 6 5 4 3 2 1

For Nancy L.,
Susan E., John R., Carol K., and Marissa M.
Thank you

Contents

Give It Up, Mom

1
My Life at a Glance

Mom waited by the front door, smoking a cigarette. I coughed on purpose, but she didn't pay any attention. She took another puff and said, "Hurry up, Rayne, or you'll be late for school. It's after eight."

"Just a sec." I stuffed the last pile of papers into my backpack.

"You could look so nice if you'd just brush the hair off your face."

My hair is long and dark brown, but never neat enough for her. We stood for a moment, looking in the mirror. We have matching brown eyes and dark skin. Since the beginning of the month I'm taller, with long legs and big shoulders like Dad.

Mom opened the door and flicked an ash outside. Emma barked and tried to squeeze by us. I blocked her way out, then inched onto the porch. Emma didn't give up easily. She lunged for the stairs, but Mom grabbed her collar. Ashes sprinkled on her back and Mom's robe.

"Why don't you quit smoking?" I asked as we brushed Emma's thick black hair.

"I will. I can quit anytime I want to."

"How about today?"

"I'll quit when I'm ready. In the meantime, worry about yourself. Your room needs cleaning. I haven't heard you practicing the piano lately. And you watch too much TV."

"There's Wendy. I have to go." Before Mom got wound up I ran across the street to my best friend.

"I can't talk to my mom anymore," I said. "All she does is tell me what I do wrong."

"That is so like parents," said Wendy. "Mine never like what I do even when they say I can decide myself."

"Tell me about it. Mom says to make my own afternoon schedule, then gets angry when I watch 'Corte Madera.'"

"Corte Madera: The Ultimate Mall" is my favorite television show. I watch it every day with Wendy and Dionna. Dionna's my other best friend. She was waiting for us at the corner.

"I can't wait to see the show today," she yelled. "I'm sure Francesca's going to invite Craig to her high school Homecoming dance."

"She'd better, or we'll go to one before her," said Wendy. "And we're only in the seventh grade."

Wendy offered us bites of her bran muffin, and for the third week in a row we walked to school making bets on when Francesca would ask Craig.

During social living class, Ms. Metzner handed back our visual media reports. Mine had a red D— on the front. In the margin was the note: "Poor ideas, poorly substantiated. Watch less TV!" I tried to prove that "Corte Madera" was socially relevant. I thought if I could convince Ms. Metzner, then Mom would have to stop complaining about my watching the show. I guessed wrong, and Mom was going to be furious.

Ms. Metzner circled around, passing out papers. Her pale gray sweater brushed my arm each time she walked by, like a cloud of bad luck. "Your papers confirmed my hunch that television rots the brain."

Several kids groaned. Dionna rolled her eyes toward the ceiling. Wendy let her tongue hang out of her mouth.

"You watch soaps or adventure programs," continued Ms. Metzner. "What happened to the news or special features?" She stopped by Wendy. "Did your parents read this?"

Wendy pulled her legs out of the aisle and said in a low voice, "No."

"I thought so," said Ms. Metzner. "They might help you select a more appropriate topic next time."

Wendy grimaced. The last thing she wanted was her parents' help. They taught classes at the state college on how to enrich children's education, and no matter what Wendy did, they tried to make it educationally worthwhile.

Ms. Metzner asked Matt Liu, "Do you know what 'coherence' means?" At least she gave me my paper in silence.

She stopped next to Dionna. "Now this paper made my day. It's clear, concise, and well written. I strongly suggest that those of you with marks below a B read it. Thank you, Dionna."

Dionna's coffee-colored skin turned chocolate-raspberry. She hates getting attention for being the smartest. Dionna wants to be a regular kid. Like me.

"Okay, class," said Ms. Metzner. "Listen up. There's more to life than television, movies, and rock videos. I want you to stop living in a vacuum. First, I want you to know what's happening in the city, the nation, and the world. Then, I want you to make a change. Make a difference you can be proud of."

Ms. Metzner's voice got higher and her face got redder. We looked at each other. We could tell she was going over the edge. I hoped she wouldn't keep us late again, because today's installment of "Corte Madera" was really important.

"The trouble with most of you is that you're not committed to anything. There's nothing you'd give your lives for." She pulled a huge box out from under her desk and dumped brochures and fliers on the Current Events table. "Here's my plan. Look at these fliers. You can fight for integration or equal pay. You can march for peace or closing nuclear power plants. You can help ban pesticides, save butterflies, coyotes, seals, whales, the waterfront, the river, or the earth.

"Take some home. Discuss your ideas with your family. Pick a cause or make your own. And by Friday tell me what you're going to do for an Impact on the World project."

Ms. Metzner was flushed and out of breath. She had us file up to the table a row at a time. That meant Wendy and I went up together — we were in row two.

Wendy whispered, "Remember when all we had to do to make our teacher happy was write a letter to our favorite author?"

I whispered back, "I care about having my ears pierced. Does that count?"

"All right, class," said Ms. Metzner, giving me and Wendy a sharp look. "Ask yourself what's the one thing you'd like to see happen."

I wanted me and Mom to be friends again.

The last buzzer sounded.

Dionna joined us as we walked past Ms. Metzner's desk. "I love this project," Dionna said. "We can do anything we want. I'm going to do Aid to the Homeless. What about you, Rayne?"

"I don't know. I'd really like to see my mom give up smoking. But I don't know if Ms. Metzner would —"

"Well, why don't you ask me?" said Ms. Metzner, coming up to us.

"I . . . uh . . ."

"I think it would be a great project. Go for it." She handed me the American Emphysema Association and the Nicotine Network brochures.

"You're lucky, lucky," said Wendy as we left school. "You're bound to get an A."

"I need it," I said, showing her the mark on my report. "There's only one problem. What if my mom doesn't want to stop smoking?"

2
"The Ultimate Mall"

Dionna, Wendy, and I walked with the other kids up to the light at Sutter and Hopkins streets. Then the three of us ran down Hopkins to my house, number 84, a blue stucco with maroon trim.

"Let's move it," I yelled. " 'Corte Madera' is about to begin."

We threw our backpacks on the hall floor. Emma came scrambling down the stairs, barking her head off. She has the loudest bark in the neighborhood. Mom says she's a great watchdog, but Dad says Emma gets away with murder. Sometimes she even barks at me. But then, she is thirteen years old.

I ran into the living room and turned on the television. The previous show was ending. Five more commercials to go. Wendy closed the blinds. Dionna and I rushed to the kitchen. She made popcorn while I poured orange

juice. We were ready before the dog in the dog-food commercial got to his bowl.

"Bet Francesca asks Craig to the dance today," I said.

"Bet she doesn't," said Wendy. "She walks by his store
every day and does nothing. What is that girl waiting
for?"

"Shhh! It's starting," said Dionna, setting a huge bowl
of popcorn on the coffee table. Emma came in and lay
down under the table.

We love the opening sequence. Everyone on the show
is there, walking along the halls or the balcony or standing in the big circle at the center of the mall, where all
the special events take place.

Francesca walks by The Locker Room and notices
Craig for the first time. He's arranging aerobic shoes in
the window. When he looks at her, he waves. She gets
embarrassed and runs to Paw, Beak, and Tail, the pet
store where she works after high school.

In the big circle, there's jazz dancing, weightlifting,
and Thai cooking demonstrations — just like real life. I
tried to explain that to Ms. Metzner in my paper but she
didn't understand.

"That's Bruce," said Wendy, pointing to a man buying coffee. "He used to run the muffin shop. Boy, his hair
looks funny. What happened to him?"

"He went to dental school," said Dionna, "while you

were visiting your grandmother last summer."

Dionna remembers everything. She even subscribes to a soap opera magazine. That's why she's the official note taker of the show. If one of us can't watch the show, another one tapes it on a VCR. But only Dionna writes in the show notebook. Someday she's going to write her own soap.

"There's Andrea, his girlfriend," said Dionna about the woman looking at kittens in the pet store window. "She still works at Voilà's. Her mom and dad want a divorce but she's trying to get them together again. Bruce told her to stay out of it. He doesn't want to get involved. But I think she should try. I would."

"Me, too," I said.

The opening sequence always ends with the sun coming up over the mall. As I said in my paper: "Night melts into dawn." The music slows down and the camera returns to Francesca walking into Paw, Beak, and Tail.

During the commercial, Wendy grabbed a handful of popcorn. Emma sat up, her eyes pleading for some. Wendy gave her a piece and she ran out in the hall to eat it.

"Francesca's got to ask him today or tomorrow," said Dionna matter-of-factly. "The ticket prices go up next week."

Francesca told Mrs. Wallenberg, the pet store manager,

that she was going to ask Craig to the dance today.

"See, I told you. I told you," said Dionna, jumping up and down, making her ponytail bounce.

We cheered when Mrs. Wallenberg told Francesca, "Go ask him now, before the stores get too busy." Emma barked in the hall, even though she knew she wasn't supposed to.

Francesca ran through the mall. Just as she got to the door of Craig's store, there was a commercial for telephones. The ad urged us to reach out and touch somebody.

"I'd use the phone," I said. "It's easier and more private. How's she going to ask him when he's working? What about all the other guys in the store?"

"She's not going to ask," said Wendy. "I told you that. This girl is going to rack up another big fat zero."

"You wait and see," said Dionna. "I have a feeling about today."

In the next commercial a woman with a huge headache held up a bottle of pills and said, "Painoff pills always help. They'll help you, too." Her smile seemed to have a thousand teeth.

"When do we get headaches?" asked Dionna, feeling her forehead.

"I'm never getting them," said Wendy.

"Me either," I said. "And I'm not taking pills. That woman's an addict. We should report her to Officer Bob."

Officer Bob came once a month to talk to our class about drug abuse.

"When my mother gets headaches," said Wendy, "she doesn't take any pills. She just lies on the couch and moans."

Nobody said anything. We all knew that.

After three commercials, for frozen foods, a diet drink, and toilet paper, "Corte Madera" came back on. Francesca was still standing outside The Locker Room.

"Go in! Go in!" we yelled. This made Emma bark her loud woofy bark as she galloped back into the living room.

"Stop it, Emma. Quiet, girl."

I held my breath as Francesca inched her way to the door. I couldn't stand the suspense. I jumped on the couch next to Dionna and buried my head under a pillow.

Wendy stamped her feet. "Do it! Do it!" she shouted. Her black hair splashed on her face with each stamp. Emma's loud woofs were beyond control.

The back door slammed and my dad poked his head into the living room. "Hey! What's going on around here? I could hear you all the way out in the garage."

3
Outrageous

The trouble with my dad is that he's home in the afternoons. He runs his own juice business, and squeezes oranges and grapefruits in our garage. In his spare time he checks up on me and my friends.

"What is this, audience participation?" asked Dad.

"Daddy, please. Francesca's going to ask Craig to the dance. Be quiet or you'll ruin it."

"*Me* be quiet — with all your noise?"

Francesca had stopped moving. She looked as if she were about to turn and run away.

"Oh, no," I said.

"Don't stop now," whispered Dionna.

Francesca looked back toward us and was replaced by a bull running through New York. This was no time for a commercial.

"I knew she wouldn't ask him. That is so like her," Wendy muttered angrily.

Dionna turned to a clean page in the notebook. "The show's not over yet."

"Why don't you girls go outside for a while?" said Dad. He had quieted Emma.

"We can't leave Francesca all alone," I said. Dad didn't understand how important Francesca was to us.

"Doesn't anyone want to help me find the recipe for perfect tomato juice?"

"Uh, no, Dad." For the last two weeks Dad has been trying to make tomato juice that tastes fresh more than one day.

"I'll split the profits."

"In that case, count me in, Mr. Provinzano," said Wendy.

"No," I said.

"Okay, I can take rejection. But I hate to see you girls watching this show. When are you going to do something significant with your lives?"

"Dad, you sound like Ms. Metzner."

"Don't your parents want you to get a Nobel Prize, Wendy? You'd better hurry up. You're getting old. You're almost thirteen. And you, Dionna . . ."

Wendy and Dionna laughed. My dad makes jokes easily and all my friends like him. He's super looking, too, with reddish-brown hair and sparkling brown eyes. He isn't tall and he isn't short — he's just right.

He doesn't pick on me as much as Mom does. He complains about my room and my grades, but he doesn't act as if I'm hopeless. The only thing he asks me to do is take care of Emma. He says that will make me responsible.

"As soon as this show is over, I want to see you all outside." Dad grabbed a handful of popcorn and returned to his tomato juice. Emma tried to follow him but he sent her back to us. "And don't forget to walk Emma."

While the three of us yelled, "No! No! Don't stop now!" Francesca hesitated another horrible moment, then turned and walked back to the pet store.

"Rats," I said.

"Wimp," yelled Wendy. "If she doesn't ask him soon, I'm going to watch another show." She banged her hand on the table.

Emma woofed a low bark. I said, "No, Emma." She crawled under the table and put her head on her paws.

"Maybe Francesca will ask him tomorrow," said Dionna.

"Sure. Keep dreaming." I stood up to stretch. "Have you decided what you're going to do your project on?" I asked Wendy.

"I'm thinking Nuclear Disarmament," she said. "But then, I might do something on Prenatal Bonding."

"What?" Dionna and I asked together.

"That's where you teach your child how to count while it's still inside you."

"Where did you hear this?" I asked.

"On a talk show," said Wendy. "But I also saw a flier at the library for a group right here in town. They're going to have a meeting this Saturday afternoon."

"Forget it, Wendy," I said. "Just drop it."

"Yeah," said Dionna. "You're asking for trouble with that topic. Even Ms. Metzner won't go for it."

On the television a man in a bar asked for a light.

"I might need another topic, too," I said. "I don't know if my mom can quit smoking."

"My dad quit cold turkey after smoking three packs a day for twenty-five years. Just like that." Dionna snapped her fingers.

On the television a bolt of lightning crashed down in the bar. The customers scattered.

"Then there's my dad," said Wendy. "Took him five years to quit."

"You're no help," I said to Wendy. "What's the big deal with cigarettes? If I want to stop something, I just stop."

"You don't understand," said Andrea. "Corte Madera" had started again. "You'll never understand." Andrea was telling Bruce she couldn't give up on her parents. Bruce was telling her she'd have to make a choice between him and them.

"Uh-oh," said Wendy. "This dude's about to split."

The camera closed in on Bruce's silent face. Jaws clenched. Eyes narrowed. He looked like a nice guy. But then, he was a dentist.

"Maybe Andrea should stick to her parents," I said.

"But she's Bruce's girlfriend," said Dionna.

"So what?" said Wendy. "I'm never going to be tied down by anyone or anything."

"You'd feel differently if you were me," said Andrea.

"But the point is, I'm not you," said Bruce. "And it's their problem, not yours or mine."

A commercial interrupted Bruce. It was for a pill to take when you don't have time to stop for the pain.

"Hi, girls. Want some cookies?" asked my mom, surprising us. "You should be outside." She reached to turn off the TV.

"Wait, Mom. We have to see Francesca go to her Homecoming dance."

Mom put a bag of groceries on the coffee table and took a handful of popcorn. "I bet she hasn't even asked him, has she?"

"Almost," I said. Mom is smart. She can watch a show for five minutes and guess what the plot is.

"Almost isn't good enough," said Mom. "She'd better hurry up. I'm getting tired of this show and the time it wastes. Even if it is in your *schedule*." Mom gave a meaningful look. She used to be happy to see me with my friends. Now she wants me to accomplish something or learn something. And if I wasn't doing any of that, then she wanted me outside. She believed that being outside would make me a better person or something.

I said, "After today we're going to be busy with projects. And mine's going to involve you. If you want."

"I'll do anything as long as it doesn't involve TV," said Mom. She picked up the groceries and went to the kitchen.

The show ended with Andrea wiping tears from her eyes. "I'll move out tomorrow," she said.

I went to the kitchen to get more orange juice. Mom was on the phone. Smoking!

"Mom! You promised not to smoke in the house."

She jumped. "I didn't hear you." Into the phone she said, "I'll have to call you back, Charlotte. Rayne's here and —"

"You said you could stop anytime you wanted!" I shouted.

"Charlotte says don't get so excited. You wait and see how much will power you have when you get to be our age."

Mom opened the window and fanned the air with a cookbook. "I'm only having a few puffs. I've had a hard day." She still had the cigarette in her hand. I grabbed her wrist and she dropped the cigarette. It rolled under the refrigerator.

"Now look what you've done," Mom said angrily. She pushed a section of newspaper under the refrigerator to move the cigarette. "It's too sticky under there. Get the yardstick, quick, before the cigarette ruins the refrigerator."

I got the yardstick. She shoved it under the refrigerator, worked it around in a circle, then pushed. The cigarette whooshed out, still burning.

Wendy and Dionna came to the doorway with the empty popcorn bowl. Emma squeezed between them.

Before I could say "Hey!" Mom picked up the cigarette and took a drag. She coughed a few times but took another puff before she threw the cigarette in the sink. Her coughs got deeper and louder. She choked.

I ran over and hit her on the back. "Give it up, Mom," I yelled. "I don't want you to die."

Mom straightened up. "Calm down. I'm fine." She poured a glass of water and drank it. She noticed Dionna and Wendy staring at her. "Isn't it time for you girls to go outside?"

Wendy's eyes widened. Dionna blushed and looked at her feet.

"Move it along, girls. I just had a little coughing fit, that's all." Mom walked past me to the door. "I'll be home by five-thirty, and I suggest you keep this to yourself."

When the front door slammed, Wendy said, "She's outrageous."

"Tell me about it," I said.

4
Three Wishes

Dad's machines filled one entire wall of our garage.
Crates of fruit were stacked everywhere else. There was
barely room for his desk. The tangy smell of fresh orange
juice made my nose itch and my mouth water.

"Dad, do you think Mom could give up smoking?"

"Yes, Pumpkin." He was filling a juicer with tomatoes.

"This year?"

"Sure. She can quit any time. The problem isn't stopping, it's staying stopped. Your mom has quit smoking
hundreds of times. Once for four days. Why all the questions?"

"We have to do a project at school, and I want to do
mine on getting Mom to quit smoking."

Dad sat down. "Hoo boy. It's one thing to help her,
but it's another to make her your school project. Weren't
you listening when I said she's stopped hundreds of
times?"

"This time will be different. Mom and I will work together. It could be a perfect project."

"Or a perfect disaster. You'd better think of some other ideas. How about me? My rise to success . . . my quest for the perfect tomato juice. Here, try this." Dad handed me a paper cup.

"I don't know . . . I'll think about it." I took a sip. "Too blah." Dad handed me another cup. "But I know one thing. I'm going to try."

"That's my girl. We Provinzanos are tough."

"This is tasty. What's in it?"

"A banana slug. See that brown swirl?"

"DAD!"

"Well, maybe a little soy sauce."

Back in my room I pushed the spare mattress, empty Pepsi can, and dirty clothes out of the way so I could lie on the floor. While I did leg stretches, I read the brochures Ms. Metzner gave me. Emma put her head on my shoulder.

A strawberry was turning into gray mold under my bureau. I thought it was gross until I read the first brochure. Cigarettes are grosser. They mess up everything inside you, from your heart to your lungs — even your brain. When I read how nicotine attacks the nervous system in only seven seconds, I knew I couldn't give up on Mom, ever. No matter what, she had to be my project.

Besides, if I helped Mom to quit, maybe she'd stop picking on me. My room could be a mess. I could wear anything I liked and never have to brush my hair. But most of all, I wished we could be like we were last year. Mom and I used to walk Emma, and Mom would tell me what she was like when she was my age.

Wendy had only one thought as she walked home: "That Rayne is one lucky girl. Her parents support her no matter what she wants to do. My parents have never liked a project I've picked. 'Let's brainstorm,' Dad says. 'What can we do to improve you?' my mother asks. Then they pick a topic and stay on my case until I do it."

Wendy hated their pushing her to get ahead. She didn't want them to devote themselves to her educational success. Last summer she threatened: "If I have to go to your summer institute, I'm not going to go to college."

Wendy didn't go to the summer institute. She became friends with Rayne and Dionna. When her parents complained about the girls' watching "Corte Madera," Wendy told her parents it was their fault because there wasn't a mall close enough to go to. The city had voted down three proposals for a mall, and each time her parents had led the fight.

Wendy turned the corner to her street, Aristotle Drive.

"What a dumb name. That's probably why my parents bought our house."

She stomped in the front door. "That you, dear?" asked her mother in a soft voice. That was another thing Wendy hated about her mother. She spoke so softly she seemed to be whispering most of the time. People said to her, "Speak up. What? I can't hear you."

"Yeah, it's me."

"Come in and tell me about your day."

"Later. I have homework to do."

Wendy made a run for the stairs, but her mother intercepted her. "What are you going to do for your Impact on the World project? I ran into Ms. Metzner at a meeting this afternoon and —"

"Mom, please. She's *my* teacher and it's *my* project."

"Okay. We can talk about it at dinner. But it had better be something more suitable than your report topic. Bumper Sticker News, indeed! What was Dionna's topic?"

"Can you leave Dionna out of this? I'm not going to become smarter from being friends with her."

"I know that," said her mother. "I just thought her topic was more appropriate. I heard Rayne's was on television and not very —"

Wendy ran upstairs to her room and closed the door. "That is just like her. Why do I have parents who find

out everything? There's no getting away from them. It
isn't fair. Why can't they leave me alone?"

Dionna had the farthest to walk. She lived two blocks
from Wendy and four from Rayne. Her house was always
noisy and filled with friends of her parents and three
older sisters.

Her mom read meters for the gas and electric company.
Between jobs she'd drive the girls to school or go by their
house to check up on everyone. Her dad ran a computer
software company at home. Clients and programmers
were always there.

The only time Dionna was alone was when she studied.
Then she had her parents' small study all to herself. Her
sisters told her to have more fun, but Dionna studied most
of the time, except when she watched "Corte Madera."

Today's show puzzled her. Why didn't Francesca ask
Craig? What did it mean when adults did things like
that? What stopped them at the last minute? If Craig
didn't want to get to know Francesca, then why did he
wave and smile at her all the time?

"Corte Madera" was important to Dionna because the
show had helped her become friends with Rayne and
Wendy. Before they started watching it together, they'd
barely talked to one another. Wendy and Rayne were

Dionna's only friends, but she didn't bring them home often. She worried that they might like her sisters better than her.

Dionna had lots of other worries. Today she worried that the Impact on the World projects might interfere with watching "Corte Madera." "If we don't watch the show, will we still be friends?"

Dionna walked up the brick steps to her house, a vine-covered gray stucco with white windows and shutters. She ran through the front hall saying "Please" each time she stepped on a tile. Dionna wished that she, Rayne, and Wendy would stay friends forever. "If I don't miss a tile, then everything will be all right." But she missed the third tile from the end.

5
Please, Mom. Mom, Mom, Mom

I was emptying the dishwasher and had four glasses in
my hands when I heard Emma's toenails click down the
stairs to the front door.

I yelled, "Hang on, Emma. I'm coming."

Emma ran back and forth to the door. She barked to
hurry me up.

"Quiet, Emma, good doggie, good girl." I opened the
door and let her out.

Emma ran down the front steps and into the yard.
When she was done, she trotted back up the steps and
sat on the porch. She likes to watch people walking by.
The trouble is, people walking by make Emma bark.

While I set the dining room table, I watched her hold
herself back when the Bossi boys and Mr. and Mrs. Fahey
went past. But when Skip Hewitt and his friends rode by
on their skateboards, Emma's sides hiccupped with woofs.
First a low woof, then louder ones.

She paused as if she knew she shouldn't bark, but then she woofed even louder when Skip and his friends walked back up the street. By the time I got to her she was woofing her head off.

"Emma, you cut that out. No bark," yelled Dad. He was in the back yard unloading oranges. Emma couldn't hear him; she was woofing about four woofs to the second.

"Hey, Rayne, Laura, somebody do something about Emma," he shouted.

"I will, Dad." I grabbed Emma by the collar. "Quiet, girl. No bark." I dragged her toward the door. "Inside. That's a good girl."

Emma looked up at me. I knew she understood I was angry. I wondered what she was thinking. As if to tell me, she woofed three low rumbly woofs, then ran inside.

"Give me a break, Emma. I need Dad to be in a good mood." I whisked her up to my room and she scrunched under my bed. I went back downstairs to finish setting the table.

I picked three roses in the front yard and put them in a vase. Mom said, "Looks nice, Rayne. Carry in the plates and we're ready to eat." She seemed to have forgotten what had happened earlier. But I hadn't.

Dad stomped in the back door. Mom and I looked at each other. We could tell the tomato juice test had not gone well. "We've got to teach that dog some manners," he said. "She's always barking."

"Relax, Ed," said Mom. "She's not that bad."

"And practically everyone on the street has a dog," I said. "Skip has three dogs."

"Dogs should learn to obey. When I was a kid we used to —"

"Ed, we've heard that before. You're the only one who cares. The neighbors are used to Emma. I'm almost used to Emma."

That was a surprise. I never knew what Mom was going to say next. To stop them from arguing, I carried the soup into the dining room. It was a minestrone, my favorite. Mom had also made focaccia bread with olive oil, sea salt, and rosemary. The smells were incredible. Dad smiled after tasting the soup.

Mom explained her new assignment at the Department of Motor Vehicles. She had to compute fines for people who'd forgotten to register their cars. Most of the people got angry when they found out how much they owed. While Mom described a woman who threatened to drive through the DMV's front door if her fine wasn't reduced, Emma came in and lay across my feet under the table. Dad gave me a look that meant "Emma better behave."

Emma behaved, and when we were laughing at one of Dad's jokes, I asked Mom to be my Impact on the World project.

"Me?" she sputtered. "Are you serious? I'm the last person in the world you want to be your project. You'd have more luck teaching Emma to stop barking when we ask her to be quiet."

Emma heard her name and ran out from under the table. I pushed her back before she could woof.

"Why not give it a try, Laura?" Dad said.

"That's easy for you to say," said Mom. "I don't see how the project can work. I'm flattered and touched, but —"

"I'm going to help," I said.

"You've helped before. Remember when you threw out all my matches and I ruined a burner on the stove lighting cigarettes? And the time you embarrassed me by throwing yourself on the floor and coughing when I lit up?"

"This time we'll work together, like a team." I handed her the brochures. "The red one has a plan for counting down to quitting day."

Mom went into the kitchen to heat up some more soup. When she came back she said, "You know, training Emma to stop barking on command would make this neighborhood more peaceful. Everyone would benefit."

"You're changing the subject," said Dad. "Not that I wouldn't like to see Emma trained."

I added, "Ms. Metzner said helping you to stop smoking would be a great project."

"I have a lot of stress in my new job."

"You always have an excuse," I said.

"I'll quit as soon as I'm ready."

"You're kidding yourself, Mom."

"Why can't you be like other kids? I bet Dionna isn't doing a project on her mother or father." When I didn't say anything, Mom said, "Find something else," and went back to the kitchen.

Dad whispered, "Don't give up. Remember, the game isn't over until it's over."

Mom came back smelling like she'd smoked. She handed me the brochures. "I've tried all these suggestions before."

"But we'll be a team and that will make a difference."

"What will happen to your grade if this project doesn't work?"

"I'll ask Ms. Metzner tomorrow. Please, Mom."

"Why can't I have a family that leaves me alone?"

"We care about you. Besides, I'll keep my room clean *and* teach Emma to bark less."

"I have to get more milk." Mom ran out to the kitchen.

"At this rate, dinner will take all night," said Dad.

The phone rang.

"How's it going?" asked Dionna.

"Not too good," I said.

"My mom's having a fit." Dionna giggled. "She thinks I'm going to bring the homeless home. She wants to know why I can't do something like you're doing. She thinks I should make my dad lose twenty pounds. My whole family's furious with me. I like it. I'm tired of being the good one."

"Dionna!"

"See? Even you expect me to be good. Call back if anything happens. Otherwise, I'll see you in the morning."

Mom was back at the table. "You and your father aren't up to my irritableness. Remember last time, when you wanted to know if I was going to get any grouchier?"

"I can handle it now, Mom."

"No, I don't think so. It would be too hard."

I jumped up and yelled. "I'm ready for anything. I want you to be my mother all my life. You have to stop smoking. Please, Mom." I got down on my knees and chanted, "Mom, Mom, Mom."

"Stop bugging me! And stop looking at me like that with your big eyes. I can't stand it."

I didn't get up. She said, "Rayne, Rayne, go away. Come again another day."

My parents always say that to get me to stop what I'm doing. And when I was younger I did stop. But not now.

"I'm not going away, Mom. Ever."

"I think she means it," said Dad.

I kept chanting "Mom, Mom, Mom."

Emma woofed as if to say, "Keep it up. You're making progress."

Mom went to the kitchen. I followed her, chanting.

She went upstairs. I followed with Emma behind me, woofing.

I even chanted into the bathroom keyhole. Ten minutes later, when my mouth was so dry I was about to fall on the floor and give up, Mom opened the bathroom door and shouted, "All right, all right, all right! I'll be your project. But don't say I didn't warn you."

6
Next on the Couch

Dad told me I was over the first hurdle, but I'd better go
easy if I wanted to stay in the race. I cleared the dining
room table so Mom and I had space to work. We went
through the brochures, picking activities Mom could do
to avoid smoking.

"I like chewing gum," said Mom, "but chewing cloves
makes me nauseous." She shivered as she thought about
them.

"Okay, I'll get gum, too." I added her favorite flavors,
peppermint and fruit, to the list of things to buy at Jim's
Drugs. So far I had:

> Toothpicks
> Nail polish
> Nail buffer
> Hair gel
> Typewriter cleaning gum

Licorice
Caffeine-free Diet Coke
Crossword puzzles
Juggling balls

It was Tuesday. Our plan was that Mom would cut down until 6 P.M. Thursday, when she'd quit. She had already changed brands and was smoking less than half a pack a day. She had enough cigarettes to last until Thursday. I wrapped a piece of paper around her pack and held it in place with a rubber band. Then I put a pencil in the band. Whenever Mom wanted to smoke, she was supposed to list the time and the reason. Also, she was supposed to try one of the activities first, to see if she could avoid smoking.

I made her a Stop Smoking chart with a "priority activity" for each day. Wednesday's was deep breathing. Thursday's was chewing gum. And Friday's was ice water.

"Thursday's the big day," said Mom. "I'll have the last cigarette of my life at six, eat dinner, keep busy until eight-thirty, then go to bed. When I wake up at seven I'll have thirteen hours of non-smoking under my belt."

"Sounds good, Mom."

"I hope so. On Friday, whenever I want a cigarette, I'll have a glass of ice water. That way I won't gain weight and it won't cost me any money. Last time I stopped I chewed a big pack of gum every day. That's fifteen pieces, one for almost every hour I'm awake. And the money I spent on gum and candy bars was more than I'd spent on cigarettes."

"This time you're going to make it."

"I hope so. Right now I'm exhausted."

I left Mom resting on the couch. She moaned a few times. Emma sat on the floor and nuzzled her arm. I called Wendy. Her mother said, "Wendy is busy studying. I'll have her call you back later." I knew that later meant never.

I dialed Dionna's number and got through with call waiting. Her sister Kafi was on the phone. She promised to tell Dionna when she was done, but that could take all night. I did my homework and thought about my project. If it was going to work, I'd need some new ideas to keep Mom from smoking.

I curled up in the big stuffed chair in my room. It was covered in green satiny material with dark wavy lines. My favorite way to think was to sit in the chair and wrap myself in the afghan Aunt Margaret made me. It was deep pink with light pink roses and green leaves. The afghan smelled like Emma, but it was warm and cozy, and I loved it. I scrunched down with a legal-size pad of yellow paper Dad had given me. He'd said, "These pads are for big ideas. Use them a lot."

I thought about Mom. She and I could become good

friends when she quit. Maybe we'd even go on a trip together. Mom could drive. Thinking about Mom driving
and how much I wanted her to quit gave me two great
ideas. First, I'd write notes that would tell Mom why she
shouldn't smoke — like saying she'd get cancer or pollute
the earth. I could put the notes everywhere: her purse,
pockets, drawers, and cabinets. That way she'd be surrounded by my help.

The other idea was to make fliers with her picture on
them, to give to people in the stores in our neighborhood.
The fliers would say not to sell Mom cigarettes. She said
one of the hardest things about quitting was to drive by
stores where she could buy cigarettes. Sometimes a little
voice made her pull over and go in. Well, now she'd have
help against that voice. I was sure she'd like this idea a lot.

I got a picture of Mom from the scrapbook. It was
taken on our vacation last summer when we were at
Castle Lake. It showed her sitting on a rock. Everyone
liked the picture. Even Mom. It looked just like her.

I passed Mom on the way back to my room. She was
on the phone talking to her best friend. "Charlotte, you'll
never guess what Rayne wants to do now . . . No, not
that. Ha! Not that either . . . She wants me to stop
smoking for her school project . . . Yes, I told her it
might not work. But you know Rayne. Doesn't take no
for an answer . . . Yes, I'm going to try. You know, she

really is a good kid. She's brave. Imagine, my kid that brave . . ."

My heart beat faster hearing Mom say that. I propped her picture against a book and started to write notes. The first one was:

Dear Mom,

You're the only mom I have and I want you to be my mom always. Please stop smoking.

Your loving daughter,
Rayne

P.S. I won't go away. Ever.

I wrote until Dad came in to say good night. I showed him the notes. He said, "This is a good idea, Rayne. You've hit on something hot."

"What's a good idea?" asked Mom, bringing laundry into my room.

"You'll see," I said, covering the notes. "It's a surprise."

The next morning I told Dionna and Wendy about the notes and the flier.

"Great," said Dionna. "If your mother quits, Ms. Metzner will have to give you an A, and you can be the smartest in the class." She burst out laughing. "My mom loathes my project. She kept saying, 'But the homeless are so dirty,' and my dad said, 'You can't go to the shelter alone.' Can you imagine? They didn't trust me. Me, Miss Responsible. And I haven't done anything yet." She laughed again.

Wendy and I looked at each other and shrugged. We'd never seen Dionna like this. She talked the rest of the way to school. "Dad said I'm going through a phase. Mom said I was becoming a teenager and was probably going to get my period."

"What about your project?" Wendy asked.

"They're going to see how it goes," said Dionna. "They're trying to be open."

"You two have all the luck," complained Wendy. "My parents were a-gi-ta-ted! They kept asking if there was another project I could do, what projects my friends were doing. We had a big fight when my mother said she was going to talk to Ms. Metzner."

"Did you tell them you were doing Prenatal Bonding?" I asked.

"No. I told them I wanted to become a Guardian Angel and ride buses to keep the passengers safe."

"Wen-dy," Dionna and I shouted at the same time.

I added, "No wonder. What happened to Nuclear Disarmament?"

"I changed my mind because I knew they'd want to go to meetings with me. I just want my parents to leave me alone. I want to pick and do my own project."

"Tell them that," I said, jumping through the fourth graders' hopscotch at the front of the school yard.

"I did," said Wendy, hopping after me. "It gave my mom a headache. She lay down on the couch and moaned."

"Hey! My mom didn't get a headache, but she lay down on the couch and moaned, too," I said.

"Our parents better buy aspirin or rent couches," said Dionna. "Because there's going to be a lot more moaning before our projects are done."

7
Pebbles in the Pond

Before class I asked Ms. Metzner, "What if my mother doesn't quit smoking?"

"Don't worry. I won't take points off your grade. I know how hard it is to stop. I don't expect nuclear disarmament or save the whales to happen by the end of your projects. I want you to make an impact, and that can be as simple as writing a letter or starting your mother on the road to quitting cigarettes. Because whatever you do will be like throwing pebbles in a pond. The ripples will cause changes all across the water, not just in the spot you threw them."

I walked away happy. I imagined Mom blowing smoke rings that became thinner and thinner until they disappeared, taking her cigarettes along with them.

During social living class we talked about our projects. Benny Levin and Bob Cooper said they were working on saving whales. "We're going to make a papier-mâché whale for the Save the Whales booth at the science museum fair," said Benny. "It's going to be so big it'll take at least a hundred hours to make."

John Rice said, "Matt and I are going to collect signatures on Greenpeace petitions. If we can use your whale to hang over our table at the Co-op supermarket, we'll help you build it."

"You're on," said Benny.

"Let's start this afternoon," said Matt.

Ms. Metzner smiled and said that their cooperative attitude was exactly what she wanted to see. "You want the world to be a better place, not just have your project succeed." Right away, everyone offered to help Brian Ortega sell chocolate-covered cherries to raise money for the Senior Center library.

Aaron Hamer said he and Brie Weisglas needed help, too. "We're going to repair a stuffed mountain lion that fell off a truck on the freeway. First we have to take out hundreds of thistles. Then we're going to learn how to replace missing fur." Only Marissa Kono said she'd help them. She transferred to our school this year and didn't know that Brie never stopped talking and that Aaron always wanted things done his way.

Kids talked about their projects all during recess and lunch. Our class hadn't been this excited since the talent show last year when a fifth-grade magician accidentally sawed the leg off a teddy bear.

On the way home Wendy said, "I've decided to do Nuclear Disarmament for my project."

"Hallelujah!" I said.

"My prayers are answered," said Dionna.

Wendy held up her hands to make us quiet. "Seiji Carpenter and Chris Lee are doing it. I could go to meetings with them. My parents would like that. I'd be kind of normal, you know?"

"You're making the right decision, girl," I said.

"And besides, Seiji's cute," said Dionna.

Wendy punched Dionna's arm.

Emma was waiting for us on the porch, thumping her tail. I patted her head and said, "You need a haircut, Emma." She rolled over and barked, then got her leash from the bottom shelf of the hall bookcase. She loved to run with me.

"Stay cool, Emma. We'll go for a run later. We have to watch the show, remember?"

Emma woofed as if she were saying yes. I got out the popcorn popper while Wendy poured juice. Dionna yelled, "It's starting."

Andrea was walking through the mall, looking very

unhappy. Above her on the upper level was Francesca, walking toward The Locker Room.

"Here we go again," said Dionna, opening the note-book.

In front of the leather store was a group of girls our age. "They're so lucky," said Wendy. "They go to the mall every day."

"And look what they're wearing," I said. "We look out of it compared to them."

"Martin, wait up!" Andrea yelled to a man carrying five large red pillows.

"Always, for you," said Martin, stopping.

Three men in jeans jackets pushed by, knocking a pillow out of Martin's arms.

"Hey! Watch it," he yelled.

Andrea picked up the pillow. "I wish my problems could be solved so easily."

"Maybe I can help." Martin moved closer to her. One of the men in jeans jackets turned around. He had long hair and looked as if he hadn't shaved in a few days.

"Okay, I give up," said Wendy. "Who's Martin?"

"A personal shopper at Voilà's," said Dionna. "He's always liked Andrea."

Good thing Dionna told us, because I'd forgotten who he was, too.

"Let's have coffee?" said Martin.

"I can't. I have to work. I'm on the sport-watch counter."

"What about tonight? I could pick you up."

"Persistent dude," said Wendy, laughing.

"Uh . . . no." Andrea looked down. Martin looked down, too. Then they looked into each other's eyes as the screen cut to a commercial for a pill to help people lose weight.

We finished off the popcorn. After commercials for chocolate chip cookies, pizza, and frozen dinners, I ran to the refrigerator and brought back two containers of yogurt for me and Wendy, and a bowl of leftover noodles for Dionna.

The show returned to Craig watching Andrea and Martin. Then it cut to Francesca, still slowly walking to The Locker Room. But this time she went inside the store. I put down my yogurt. Wendy sputtered. Dionna stopped slurping noodles and grabbed a pen. "I don't believe it," she mumbled.

"What can I do for you?" asked Craig, rubbing his jaw.

"Just looking," said Francesca. She walked over to a sale box and picked up a visor. "I'll take this for my dad."

I yelled, "Okay, now the dance. Ask him to the dance!"

Craig put the visor in a box. "Anything else?" he said.

"Yes. Would you . . . could you . . ."

"Yes?" asked Craig, looking into her eyes.

"I can't stand it," said Dionna. "She's got to ask him."

Craig put a bag of ice on his cheek.

"What's the matter?" asked Francesca.

"If he dies or gets any sickness that prevents him from going to the dance, I'm suing," I said.

"Really," said Wendy.

"Nothing . . . just a sore tooth." Craig moaned softly.

"How did he get a sore tooth?" asked Wendy.

"You'd better see your dentist," said Francesca. She pointed to the front case. "Could I see those bowling socks?"

"What about the dance?" I made faces at the screen to urge her on.

"I hate to say this," said Wendy, "but sometimes this show makes me want to work on my project."

"Me, too," said Dionna, snapping the notebook closed.

Francesca bought the socks and a sweat band, and was looking at warm-up suits when the next commercial came on.

The show returned to the three men in jeans jackets. The one with long hair went into Voilà's housewares department. The other two waited for him outside the main door. The man with long hair took the elevator to the second floor, walked down the employees' hall, and pushed open the door to the store manager's office.

"This is new," I said.

"No, they planned this meeting last month when you

went to have your eyes examined," said Dionna. She flipped through the notebook. "Yeah. Here it is. They're after the spring buying contracts. They're worth big money to certain people."

The camera cut back to Francesca walking through the mall with a huge package. "She went berserk shopping," said Wendy. "I bet she bought a bowling ball and a punching bag."

"What about the dance?" I yelled again.

Craig said to the other salesmen, "I felt she wanted something else."

"How sensitive," said Wendy.

"She likes you," said a salesman. "She walks by every day. I'm telling you she likes you. And you need a girl-friend."

"I need a dentist," Craig moaned.

"Try this guy." The salesman handed Craig a card. The closing credits flashed on the screen, superimposed on Bruce's business card.

I showed Dionna and Wendy the notes. "I'm going to put them around the house tomorrow night after Mom quits."

"Call me if you need help," said Wendy. "I have to tell my parents about my new project. If they don't let me go to tonight's meeting, I'll join Aaron and Brie and we'll work on the mountain lion in my living room."

After Dionna and Wendy left I worked on my flier. I

pasted Mom's picture on a piece of paper and used fat marking pens to write:

I went to the copy center and made a hundred fliers. Let other kids throw pebbles. I was going to start an avalanche.

8
On the Road

I went first to the Derby Street Market. Five brothers ran
the store. The oldest brother, Nick, was there, smoking.
He was a short, muscular man with bushy eyebrows. He
read the flier and coughed. "You're something else. You
sure this is okay with your mother?"

"Yes. She said I could help her stop smoking. Will you
take one?"

"Since you've been such a great customer." He taped
the flier next to the cash register, by the book of charge
card numbers he couldn't accept. "I'll remind her she's
supposed to be quitting. What she does after that is up to
her. I can't refuse to sell her cigarettes."

"Even if she said I could help her stop?"

"Right, it's a free country. But I have a hunch this will
stop her. And who knows? Maybe it will get me to cut
down." He laughed and stamped his cigarette out.

Next stop was Seven Palms. Lev Zucker was on the

main cash register. He was a tall, handsome man with blue eyes and runaway gray hair. "Oh, my," he said when he looked at the flier. "I hope no one does this to me." I must have looked disappointed because he quickly added, "But I wish someone loved me enough to do it." He pinned the flier next to his cash register. "Don't worry. It's a good thought."

At Jim's Drugs I bought the stuff on Mom's list. Rita Valvano, Mom's and my favorite checker, said, "Your idea's great. We're not supposed to do things like this, but I'll take care of it." She grabbed ten fliers.

At Safeway and Co-op the managers wouldn't take the fliers because checkers couldn't refuse to sell adults cigarettes. "Even if they could," said Mr. Brown at Co-op, "they already have enough to do looking up prices and bagging. But I'll tell you one thing: I wish I tried this on my dad. He died of lung cancer and I miss him. You're a good kid to do this for your mother. I hope she appreciates you." He took a flier and said he'd keep an eye out for Mom.

Two blocks away Wendy was thinking about nuclear disarmament. Even though she hadn't told anyone, she worried about what would happen if the Russians attacked. Most people said it would happen in her lifetime. She wondered why her parents never talked about it.

Ms. Metzner said the world could become a better place if everyone cared and did something. Dionna and Rayne believed that. But Wendy wasn't sure if she did.

She wanted to give her project a try, but she didn't want to go to meetings with her parents. They might let her go with Seiji and Chris. The only other possibility was to go with her grandmother. She was coming on Friday to stay for a few weeks. Her visits put both parents on the couch. Wendy could say she was helping her parents by taking her gandmother to a meeting. They might even be grateful. Wendy found that thought shocking. The only problem was, she didn't know what her grandmother would think.

Mom was on the phone when I got home. "It's after six, Rayne. I was beginning to worry."

"I'm fine, Mom. Sorry I'm late."

"Charlotte says you can have her for a project if I don't work out."

"No thanks, Mom. You're all I want."

"But Charlotte's ready to give up chocolate, television, or coffee. You get to name it."

"I already did."

"Seems to me you're turning down a good deal."

"Right, Mom." I ran to my room and hid the fliers in my desk. When I came back she said, "Today I tried deep breathing. It helped, but I'm dreading Friday."

"You can do it." I hugged her. "Ms. Metzner said my grade doesn't depend on your quitting but on the work I do to help you to stop."

"That's a relief," said Mom.

Dad came in from the garage with a thermos hanging from each shoulder. He filled two paper cups. "Try this."

Mom tossed hers down. "Agg! Argh! This could get me to stop anything."

I didn't want to swallow mine, but Dad was looking at me. I couldn't hurt his feelings, so down it went. "Yuk!" I yelled. The juice was so bad it almost came back up. "What's in that?"

"A professional secret."

"Better keep it a secret," said Mom.

"I will if you try this." He unscrewed the top of the other thermos.

"No, no," Mom and I both yelled. I ran to set the table and Mom said, "I've got to check the rice."

We left Dad standing there, mumbling, "This is support? This is gratitude? Do I have to do it all? Shoot the baskets *and* get the rebounds?"

During dinner Mom said that everyone at work wished her good luck and said they'd help. I gave her everything I bought at Jim's Drugs. Dad surprised her with a red leather journal. "Use this to keep track of what you do and how you feel," he said. "Then you can write a book about how you stopped."

Right there I felt we were a perfect family. We all helped each other. Then I got a great idea about the journal becoming a book. "We could go on television," I shouted. "And you can say how *I,* Rayne Provinzano, your wonderful daughter, helped you to stop smoking."

Mom smiled. "You guys are incredible. I haven't quit yet."

Still, if she kept a journal and wrote a book, I just knew we could go on television. That happened all the time.

After dinner Mom went over to Charlotte's to help her hem a pair of pants. Dad went to the garage to work on his tomato juice. I called Wendy and told her about the problem with the fliers. "The checkers can't refuse to sell Mom cigarettes."

"Offer a reward," said Wendy. "Then you'll know when she has cigarettes and you can confiscate them."

"Good thinking," I said. "But what about the fliers I already have?"

"Write 'Wanted, dead or alive' on them."

"Dead? I don't want Mom dead. That's the whole point of my project."

"Don't get excited," said Wendy. "Saying 'dead or alive' will make people notice your flier."

"Maybe, but I only have eighteen dollars."

"So offer five," said Wendy. "I have to leave for the meeting. Mom's going to drive and pick me up. I told her Chris and Seiji would be there, so she promised to stay in the car."

I called Dionna. She liked Wendy's idea and suggested, "Write 'Reward' on the fliers and offer three dollars."

"What about the fliers I already made?"

"Try taping a piece of paper on them with the new information."

I did and it worked. My flier now looks like this:

All I had to do was fix the rest of the fliers and pray that I didn't get more than six calls.

9
Crossing the Line

"My mother stayed in the car," said Wendy as the three of us walked to school the next morning. "But the meeting was *bor-ing*, really *boring*."

"Even with Chris and Seiji there?" I asked.

"They're infants," said Wendy. "They'll volunteer to do anything. The meeting was about a bus ride to Sacramento. All anyone talked about was who was going to be in charge of portable toilets or paper cups. The organizers were glad to see me because they had a million things I could do, like Xerox, pack fliers —"

"What did you expect?" I asked. "To dismantle missiles?"

"I want to do something important. How can I say I made a mark on the world if all I do is bring toilet paper to Sacramento?"

Dionna rolled her eyes. "Join my project."

"Nahhh, I don't want to get involved with the homeless. It's not exciting. You know what I mean?"

"Wen-dy," I shouted. "We're supposed to be helping people." She was being a real pain today.

"You help the homeless. I want to do something else." Wendy looked through brochures and somehow managed to walk, talk, and read at the same time.

"I don't want to go to Sacramento. I want something I can do right here in town."

"What about the cancer society or the AIDS hospice?" I asked.

"No, they're too . . . too depressing."

"I'm glad I don't have to depend on *you* for help," I said.

"Don't be judgmental," said Wendy.

"Look who's talking," said Dionna.

"Wait, hold on. I think I found something." Wendy stopped to show us a brochure. "Yes, this is it. This is really it."

"Let me guess — power dreaming?" I asked.

"Better than that. I'm going to make our city a Nuclear Free Zone." Wendy narrowed her eyes. "All I have to do is collect sixteen-thousand signatures to put the initiative on the ballot."

"That's all *you* have to do?" Dionna shrugged. "Hey, go for it."

"Well, other people are going to help, too," said Wendy.

"And they've already started. But this is the project for me."

"I've heard that before," I said. Wendy was getting to be as bad as Francesca about changing her mind.

"Really," insisted Wendy. "Tonight's a meeting. You wait and see."

She ran ahead of us into the school yard. As soon as we got there, Maya Montali and Carley Allen asked Dionna what had happened to Francesca on the show.

During social living, Maya and Olivia Dunn said they were going to raise money for a Nicaraguan child care center. They had pictures of the kids. "We're going to sell jewelry and pottery at a fair this weekend," said Maya.

When Morgan Buttnick said he was going to work on Aid to the Homeless, Dionna pretended she was gagging. At recess she said, "What a drag. He's always trying to talk to me."

"You don't have to do things with him, do you?" I asked.

"I hope not."

Wendy told everyone she was going to make our city the largest voter-approved Nuclear Free Zone in the United States. By the time we got to my house after school, I'd heard enough about the Nuclear Free Zone to last me all year. I was ready for Francesca. Luckily, she was first on the show. She gave her father the visor and bowling socks. He looked surprised.

"I bet he doesn't even bowl," said Wendy.

Francesca went to her room and pulled a blue flowered dress out of a shopping bag.

"Hey, look at that," said Dionna. "She bought a dress for the dance."

Francesca turned slowly in front of the mirror.

"She looks great," I said. "I wish it were mine."

"Me, too," said Dionna. "I wonder what she's going to do with her hair. It would look good pulled off her face." Dionna showed us what she meant with her own hair.

Francesca unfolded a piece of paper. The camera closed in to show:

CRAIG   831-9322

"At last," I said.

"Oh, call, call," whispered Dionna.

"If she does, I'll pass out," said Wendy.

We held our breath until an advertisement for a movie interrupted. The hero kept stopping in the middle of fights to stare at the woman he loved.

"Wow," said Dionna. "Intense."

The show returned to Bob and Kate. They were always at the beach and always kissing. Some days they would get ready to go home but then find an excuse to stay on the beach. Other days they would go home but come back that night. I liked them because they wore bathing suits, and once they even went in the water.

"Their lips are going to fall off," said Wendy.

"Don't they ever get hungry?" I asked. I ran into the kitchen and brought back a bowl of apples and a plate of ginger snaps.

As if she'd heard me, Kate squirmed free and got a picnic basket. Bob wrapped a blanket around them. They took turns feeding each other bites of chicken and pieces of cheese.

"This is heaven," said Kate.

"You're my heaven," said Bob, kissing her wrist.

"Where is Francesca?" demanded Wendy.

Even though I liked Bob and Kate, I wanted to get back to Francesca, too. Calling Craig was the moment we were waiting for. But the show cut to the mall. Andrea was showing Martin watches. The long-haired man in a jeans jacket walked past them to the men outside. He said, "The safe's in there, all right. They'll have the information we want Friday."

"See? I told you," said Dionna.

At The Locker Room, Craig's tooth was worse. He called Bruce. We yelled, "No," and "Don't do it," but Craig made an appointment. Emma growled when Bruce appeared on the screen, hovering over a patient. The sound of drilling made me shiver.

Bruce said, "You know, Carla, in spite of your overbite, you're very pretty."

"He's not wasting any tears over Andrea," said Wendy.

"Mmpfgh," said Carla.

"Who's Carla?" I asked.

"Big Al's wife," said Dionna. "He runs Al's Big and Tall Shop in the mall."

"Oh, yeah," I said.

"Bruce is disgusting," said Wendy.

At last Francesca returned. She was sitting in the chair by her phone. The show ended with Francesca staring at the number and us yelling, "Call! Call!"

We carried our dishes into the kitchen and I checked the answering machine. There was a message for Mom from Charlotte and two for Dad about juice deliveries.

As we left the house Dionna said, "I have to deliver fliers."

"When do you get to meet some homeless people?" I asked.

"Saturday morning. I'm going to help in the breakfast kitchen. Until then, I'll be distributing fliers. I hate it when people who don't like the homeless yell at me as if it's my fault or something."

"Get Morgan to help," said Wendy.

"Please, I don't need him. Where are you going, Wendy?"

"To the Nuclear Free Zone office. And stop laughing, you two. I'm sure this is the project for me."

"The perfect project," I teased.

"How are you going to convince your parents to let you go to another meeting?" Dionna asked.

"Wait and see," said Wendy. "Just wait and see."

We split at the corner. I went to the supermarkets. At the Co-op Mr. Brown liked the changes I'd made and let me give the reward flier to the checkers. But at the Safeway I had to put the flier on the bulletin board.

I ran into Dionna in the parking lot. "I feel like I've been delivering fliers all my life," I said. "If this keeps up, we won't have time to watch our show."

Dionna gasped. "Don't say that."

"We won't miss anything. By the time we're done, I bet Francesca still hasn't called Craig."

"But we have to see each other," said Dionna. "We could tape the show and watch it together."

"Yeah. Maybe. Let's talk about that with Wendy."

I left Dionna standing there, saying, "O-kay!" She looked worried. I hoped her parents weren't bugging her about her project.

"O-kay," Dionna repeated slowly and softly. They had to watch the show together. Otherwise, she wouldn't see

Rayne and Wendy. Dionna didn't know how Wendy felt, but she knew Rayne liked her. Only, she was sure Rayne liked Wendy better. Wendy was funnier. In fact, everyone was funnier than she was, and that scared her.

Dionna wished they could work on the same project. But she didn't want to work on Rayne's project because she didn't believe Rayne's mother could quit smoking. And she didn't think Wendy was going to stick to the Nuclear Free Zone. That meant she had to ask them to switch to Aid to the Homeless with her. Why was everything becoming so complicated?

As she walked into her house Kafi yelled, "Dionna, hurry up. Wendy's on the phone. Her mom's on the couch again."

I arrived back when Mom did. "My jaw hurts," she said. "I went through six packs of gum."

"Did it help?" I asked.

"For not smoking, sure. But my teeth might not be able to take it."

Mom grumbled while we got dinner. I made a salad, garlic bread, and spaghetti. I even helped sauté onions and peppers for the sauce because I knew she was nervous about tonight. Finally, it was six o'clock. Dad came in from the garage and suggested we do a ritual or something to mark Mom's giving up smoking.

We broke up all Mom's cigarettes and made a circle of tobacco on the floor. Mom stood in the center and smoked the last cigarette of her life.

"It's hard to enjoy it with you guys looking at me," she said.

"Do you want us to leave, Laura?" Dad asked.

"Yes, please. I want to finish the rest by myself. I want to make peace with the smoker inside me."

I liked that. Mom had to let go of all those parts of her that made her smoke.

She called us back when she was done. We danced around the kitchen, yelling, "Hey! Out! Begone!" Anything we could think of that would make the cigarette ghosts go away. Emma jumped around us, woofing.

"Here's to your success," said Dad, pouring a bottle of sparkling apple juice.

"Here's to the new you," I said to Mom.

"And the new you," she said to me as we tapped glasses.

Emma woofed again.

I didn't know it then, but with that toast Mom and I crossed a line we could never cross back over.

10
Wait for the Beep

After Mom went to bed Dad helped me hide the notes. We put them in her purse, bureau drawers, socks, and coat pockets. I even put one in her rain boots. And Dad put one in the medicine cabinet. At the same time I threw out matches. I saved only one package, for the fireplace.

In the morning I said to Mom, "Good luck. If you need me, I'll come home from school."

"Don't plan on it," she said.

I didn't plan on it, but I wished she would call. I was barely able to concentrate during school. I couldn't stop wondering how she was doing.

After school I almost went by the DMV to check on her. I was glad I had to watch the show.

"Francesca's never going to call Craig," complained Wendy. "Forget her doing anything."

"I don't know," said Dionna. "I think she will."

"I can't think of anything but Mom," I said.

We had to wait until Francesca came on. Bob and Kate had salad, vegetables, dessert, coffee, and three thousand kisses. Carla slapped Bruce. The men in jeans jackets planned their robbery. And Martin bought a stopwatch.

When the show cut to Francesca, she was still sitting by the phone, staring at Craig's number.

"Girl, you're going to die in that chair," said Wendy.

Dionna and I screamed, "Call!"

Emma ran in and looked around to see if anyone had sneaked in the house.

Slowly, Francesca dialed Craig's number. She got his answering machine and recorded rap: "Hi, my name is Craig and you got my line. I'm not in, but my dog'll do fine." There was loud woofing, which made Emma run over to the television set and sniff. Craig continued: "Tell him all you want me to know, and I'll call you right back, I'm not a no-show." After another woof we heard: "Now don't be a creep. Wait for the beep."

"This is someone she wants to ask out?" said Wendy. "This is what we've been waiting for?"

Emma turned and sat with her back to the television set.

Francesca cleared her throat twice. "Hi, I'm Francesa — I bought bowling socks today. Remember? The blue ones? I also bought a visor — the kind that were on sale. I was wearing a gray jacket — with a zipper — and a red stripe on the cuffs."

"Oh, give it up," moaned Dionna, putting her head in her hands.

"Get to the point," I shouted. "Next thing, she'll be telling him what she had for breakfast."

"I go to your old high school and I'm a junior. I was in your Spanish class two years ago. I work at the mall, at the pet store. Anyway, I want to ask you to — the — uh — Homecoming dance. I'll get the tickets."

"Next, she'll be telling him she'll pick him up," I said.

"I can drive. And there's going to be a live band. So if you want to go, please call me at 526-7259. Also, please call if you don't want to go, because I have to know — you know? Okay? Did I say I was, I mean, I am Francesca?" The machine cut her off. She groaned as she hung up. "I ruined it. He's going to think I'm a jerk. What am I going to do?"

"Leave town," said Wendy.

Dionna and I shook our heads.

We all went upstairs to my room. Emma, too, carrying a plastic bone in her mouth. She scrunched under my bed and gnawed on the bone.

"This is a tough day for everyone," I said. "Mom quit smoking last night."

"I'll keep my fingers crossed that she makes it," said Dionna, straightening up my desk.

"Cross them for me, too," said Wendy. "I'm going to

have a hard day. My grandmother comes this afternoon. Dad's picking her up at the airport."

"So?" said Dionna. She hung up my best sweater and put my hightops in the closet.

"She's going to be my ticket out of the house. My parents approve of the Nuclear Free Zone as a project, but they want me to go to the meeting with an adult. I want that adult to be Grandma."

"You would," I said.

Dionna looked at Mom's Stop Smoking chart and suggested, "Have her do exercises and give her rewards. That helped my dad."

"Rewards helped my dad, too," said Wendy. "Except sometimes he kept on smoking and wouldn't return the rewards, no matter what my mom said."

"Let's fill out this chart through next week," said Dionna. "She won't feel like doing it tomorrow. She'll be screaming for a cigarette."

The new chart read:

Saturday	Sunday	Monday	Tuesday
Do jumping jacks	Buff & polish nails	Eat licorice	Play with typewriter gum

Wednesday	Thursday	Friday
Apply hair gel & mousse	Throw juggling balls	Chew gum

"What's typewriter gum?" asked Dionna.

"This purple stuff." I tossed her a piece. "It's like play dough and it comes in great colors."

"Don't forget: smell her breath, check her purse for matches, and ask her friends if they've seen her smoking," said Wendy.

"That's treating her like a criminal."

"Has she ever lied to you about her smoking?" asked Wendy.

"Yes. But that was last year. Do I have to be so suspicious now?"

"Yes," said Dionna. "Otherwise, you'll be sorry."

"And if you do something stupid, tell her it's because you breathed her smoke and now you're retarded," said Wendy. "That'll really get to her."

I hadn't bargained for this when I asked my friends for help. I sat and listened to Wendy until Dionna said, "We have to talk about the show." Her voice quavered. "We're going to be busy with our projects: going to meetings, delivering fliers, and other stuff. We won't be able to watch the show together every day."

"We'll take turns taping it," I said.

"Or watch it alone," said Wendy.

"Wen-dy!" I said. She liked to tease Dionna. And Dionna looked very unhappy. "Don't worry," I said. "We'll watch the tape together. Won't we, Wendy?"

"Yeah, I guess so," said Wendy. "I'd miss you both even if you are retarded from your parents' smoking."

Dionna and I buried her in pillows and made Emma jump on top.

11
Ice Water Torture

Mom staggered into the house. "It was tough, really tough. But I didn't smoke. Not even a puff."

I jumped and yelled, "Yay! I knew you could."

"It wasn't easy. I drank so much water I had to keep going to the bathroom. And because I was gone from my desk so much, the line in front of my window stretched all the way to the main office. Even with Sheryl and Rose from Licenses helping, the line moved slowly and people were furious. I don't think I can take another day like today."

"Yes, you can, Mom," I said.

"It was torture. I don't ever want to see another piece of ice again." She threw her coat on a hook in the hall and slumped on a kitchen stool. She put her head in her hands and groaned. "Lord. Oh, Lord, do I want a cigarette."

"No, you don't. You look healthier already. And you

don't smell smoky. See how much difference one day makes?"

Her groans got louder. Emma nuzzled her knees. "You have no idea what it's like," she said. "I think I'm going to die."

"You can't. Not now. Dad's getting a pizza." I hugged her, then finished setting the table. Mom didn't move the whole time, even when I asked if she wanted anything. This was not like her. At all. "Maybe you should call Charlotte," I said. Mom still didn't move, so I dialed the number for her.

Dad came in while she was talking. He said, "This is just the beginning. We've got to hang tough. If we fumble the ball now, the game's over."

"What about a reward?" I asked. "Wendy and Dionna say rewards are important."

"Let's take her to a movie," said Dad.

Mom liked the idea, and we left for the theater right after dinner. On the way Mom said, "I loved your notes, Rayne. They helped me through a lot of tough spots. After lunch I seriously considered throwing in the towel. I even asked Rose for a cigarette."

"You didn't." I gasped.

"I was having a hard time. But then I put my hand in my coat pocket and found this note." She pulled it out and read:

Dear Mom,
    Your lungs are BLACK *from smoking. Don't*
you want them to be PINK? *I do. So* QUIT SMOKING.
                                        Your only daughter,
                                        Rayne

"That note saved me. I told Rose to keep her cigarettes.
You really helped. Thanks."
    Every part of me felt warm and good. Mom and I were
a team. Just like I wanted us to be.

12
G.T.

I hated being suspicious of my own mother, but I knew
Dionna and Wendy were right: I had to keep Mom under surveillance. Saturday morning I got up at six A.M.
so I'd know when she got up. While I waited I made a
list of chores to do: clean my room, empty wastebaskets,
bring dirty clothes downstairs, start a wash, and give
Emma a bath.

Wendy was going to come over early and help me
wash Emma. Dionna was coming over after she went to
the breakfast kitchen. I started cleaning my room. I was
careful and quiet and took only one break, to get a banana. At seven o'clock, Mom got up. I followed her downstairs. I went out for the newspaper and saw Dionna
walking to the kitchen. I waved to her.

Dionna didn't see Rayne. She was in a hurry to get to the
breakfast kitchen. Walking up Telegraph Avenue that
early scared her. The people who had slept in the park

looked mean and desperate, with beady eyes, wobbly legs, and pinched faces. Some looked as if they hadn't washed in days. Dionna knew that looking grubby didn't mean that someone would be violent, but it made them look like they might be. They looked like the people her parents warned her about when they said, "Don't get into a stranger's car. Don't let a stranger touch you."

At the end of the park there were buckets of water for the homeless to wash with. The sun was coming up over the treetops. No fog or clouds. Just clear gray sky.

Dionna recognized a man on the corner. He stood as still as a statue, with his hand held out for money. She'd seen him in front of the library and in the Clean Scene Laundromat. He had a paper bag on his head. Why would an adult do that? Why couldn't he find a job? She wondered if this could happen to her parents. Could it happen to her?

Dionna said hello and received the barest flicker of recognition. She continued to the kitchen, where she was told to set out containers of sugar and milk. Then the doors opened for people to come in. Soon the man with the paper bag on his head stood in front of the counter where she was scooping oatmeal into bowls. He wore a blue zippered sweat shirt with two white stripes on the arms. His eyes looked washed out and tired, as if he'd had the flu.

He took as much food as he could get, didn't smile, and

ate alone by the window underneath the stairs. Outside, sunlight streamed through the trees into the courtyard. It was going to be a bright, wonderful day. But Dionna knew that for the people in the kitchen the day wouldn't be bright or wonderful.

Dionna went to Rayne's after the breakfast. Rayne's mom was in the living room doing jumping jacks. "Rayne's upstairs giving Emma a bath," she called out between shouting "Twenty-eight" and "Twenty-nine."

Wendy and I were rubbing Emma dry with towels when Dionna arrived. Emma made happy moans and nestled in our arms. The smell of her tar shampoo pierced the air. And there were wet footprints everywhere.

Dionna told us about her morning. "The staff is great. They want me to come back. The hard part is seeing homeless people I think I know but really don't. Like this guy with a paper bag on his head — I couldn't think of anything to say to him that didn't sound dumb."

"I know what you mean," I said. "I always feel embarrassed because I have so much."

"If you could get him to take the bag off his head, that would be a terrific mark on the world," said Wendy.

"WEN-DY!" I yelled.

"That's okay," said Dionna. "Maybe I will. I know his name now. He's called G.T. We have to help him."

13
Not Me

Wendy and Dionna stayed until Mom took a nap Saturday afternoon. When she got up I started a new strategy: I walked by her and smelled her clothes and breath. I didn't smell any smoke. All I smelled was orange juice. Mom said she was drinking a lot to flush nicotine out of her system. When I asked if she was smoking, she said loudly, "No! Not me."

She also said, "My legs aren't up to any more jumping jacks, either." She moved ahead on her chart and got out her favorite nail polish: Amber Flame. She polished and buffed her nails four times. Then, after a bowl of popcorn, three glasses of mineral water, and a package of diet chocolates, she spent the rest of Saturday cleaning out. She didn't skip a closet, cabinet, or storage area.

I watched her throw out Dad's hippie pants, Aunt Marion's slide rule, and the six-foot wooden fork and spoon Charlotte bought in Hawaii. I thought Mom was getting carried away, but Dad said, "Leave her alone. She's building a strong base so she can go the distance."

Sunday night Dionna came over to do homework. Wendy arrived later after getting petitions signed.

"Have enough signatures yet?" I asked.

"I got thirty-seven yesterday and forty-nine today. So don't laugh. My grandmother helped. We made a pact to stick together. We went to a meeting last night by ourselves and we're going to a potluck tomorrow."

There was a loud thump downstairs.

"That's Mom," I said. "She's gone over seventy-two hours without smoking."

"Sounds like she's moving the furnace," said Wendy.

"She could be," I said. "She's moved everything else."

"Be careful," said Wendy. "She could smoke a cigarette any moment. Keep checking on her."

"But I have been, and she said —"

"I want to show you something," said Dionna. She took us to the living room and loaded a show tape into the VCR. She fast-forwarded to the middle of the opening. "See anything suspicious?"

"No," I said, looking carefully.

"See that woman under the escalator?"

"It's Carla," said Wendy.

"She's smoking!" I yelled.

I was surprised I'd never noticed this. But Dionna had watched the show since its beginning over a year ago.

"She told everyone she'd stopped smoking," said Dionna.

"My dad did that," said Wendy. "But when he ran errands, he came back smelling of smoke."

"How come you didn't tell me about Carla before?" I asked.

"I didn't remember until last night and you had enough to handle with your mom's first day of quitting."

"Carla reminds me of my aunt," said Wendy. "She'd order deliveries from the grocery store on days when she was working at home. She said she had to get fresh meat for my uncle's dinner, but she always included a pack of cigarettes. My uncle figured out what she was doing and told the store not to deliver anymore."

"Mom isn't smoking," I insisted.

"Do you have proof?" asked Wendy.

"What more do you want? She said she isn't smoking and she doesn't smell like she's smoking. The only thing left is to read her journal."

"Not a bad idea," said Dionna.

Wendy nodded.

"No! You can't mean that. I can't read Mom's journal. Not me."

"Why not?" asked Dionna.

"Yeah, really," said Wendy.

"It's private. She and Dad and I just had a long talk about privacy and they agreed to stay out of my room no matter what. And now she's my project and we're going to be a team. So I can't."

"Okay, okay. Calm down," said Dionna. "The journal's there if you need it."

14
The Muffled Scream

On Monday in social living Ms. Metzner said, "Now that you all have a project, I want to know how it's progressing. So starting today I want to hear oral reports."

Some kids moaned, but she said, "It's not difficult. Just tell me what you're doing. To prepare, get a notebook and write down what you do on your project each day. And yes, I know that some days you won't do anything. This is a good opportunity to learn how you work."

Some kids hate writing in a notebook, and I'm one of them.

"Keep the entries simple, and bring your notebooks every day so I can read them."

This time the whole class groaned.

"Don't worry. I only want a five-minute report. Each day we'll hear four or five."

Shannon McCollem went first. Her project was Dance for Peace. She'd twisted her ankle and wondered if she should change to another project. Ms. Metzner said she should change only if she wanted to. "I'm sure you can work on posters or help in another way until your ankle is better."

Aaron went next and talked way longer than five minutes about how to replace missing fur on a stuffed mountain lion. Ms. Metzner cut him off when half the class put their heads down on their desks.

While Bob and Benny described their progress on the papier-mâché whale, Ms. Metzner handed me a newsletter with a calendar entry circled in red. On the way home, I told Dionna and Wendy, "Each Tuesday afternoon there's a meeting for children of smokers at the National Society for Stopping Smoking. Should I go tomorrow?"

"Definitely," said Dionna. "I can tape 'Corte Madera.'"

"Go," said Wendy. "We'll work out when to watch the show later."

We stopped at Jim's Drugs to buy notebooks.

"These projects sure are keeping you busy," said Rita, our checker.

"Too busy," said Dionna.

We got back to my house in time for the show. Francesca was walking through the mall. When she saw Craig waiting for her in front of the pet shop she said, "Oh, no. He's heard the message. I can't face him." She turned and ran.

"Stop! Wait!" Craig yelled and ran after her. She cut through Al's Big and Tall Shop. Carla got excited and pulled a cigarette out from behind the receipt book.

When the commercials came on, we argued over what Francesca should do. During the ad for soup, our consensus was for Francesca to keep running; but during the ad for air freshener, our consensus was for her to stop.

Francesca ran through Voilà's country kitchenware, cutting around designer sleepwear, and racing past the sportwatch counter, where Andrea was showing Martin and one of his clients how to set the countdown alarm on a jogging watch. Andrea was startled to see Francesca running and dialed Security. When Craig ran by she gave the phone to Martin and ran after them.

Francesca reached the door marked Employees Only and turned to see Craig closing in. She opened the door and ran down the hall to the first office, where the men in jeans jackets were stuffing papers into a suitcase. She screamed but the man with long hair put his hand over her mouth, muffling her screams. Craig rushed in and was hit on the head. He fell to the ground, unconscious.

The man dragged Francesca, screaming muffled screams, out of the office and down to the garage. Andrea followed cautiously, using the freight elevator. She took cover behind a stack of cartons and wrote down the license plate as the car with Francesca inside knocked down a guard, smashed through the toll gate, and screeched out into the night.

"Wow," said Dionna. "That's hot."

"Yeah, really," said Wendy.

"*Our* lives are never going to be that exciting," I said.

"You want excitement?" said Mom, stomping into the room and turning off the television set. "I'll give you excitement, because I am FURIOUS!"

We sat up straight, fast.

"Just whose idea was it to make that flier that's all over town?"

"Mine," I said softly. "But —"

"NO BUTS! I was not thrilled to discover myself on a poster at the checkout stand at the Seven Palms. Do you have any idea how embarrassing that was?"

"But, Mom —"

"There I was, asking for one, just one, lousy pack of cigarettes, and the clerk wouldn't sell me any. He pulled out a flier and waved it around for everyone to see."

"But Mom, you gave up smoking last week."

"That is no reason to humiliate me. I had enormous difficulties today. ENORMOUS. None of the methods helped. Today's was eating licorice, and look at my tongue. I bet it's black down to my toes. All I needed was one cigarette. And what did I get? HUMILIATION, that's what. Where did you get such an idea?"

"You liked the notes. I got —"

"Those notes! I've had enough of those notes. They were cute at first, but ENOUGH." She threw a note on the floor. Emma ran over to sniff it, then ran back to lie on the rug. "I don't want you to pull a stunt like that again. Do you understand me?"

"Yes, Mom." I hoped she'd calm down soon.

"Did you get a cigarette?" asked Wendy. She never knew when to be quiet.

"NO, I DIDN'T. It's time you went home."

Wendy and Dionna grabbed their stuff and ran to the door. Wendy said she'd call later. "Good luck," said Dionna.

Mom kept complaining. "I went into the Co-op and Mr. Brown told me he'd heard about my not smoking. Have you been everywhere?"

"Yes. Because you promised to stop. You did. We broke all your cigarettes. Remember?"

"Really, Rayne, you just don't have any idea what it's like." She sat on the couch. She looked tired. "I want you to get the fliers back from the stores."

"No."

"Don't say no to me, I'm your mother."

"You said you'd quit. You said you could stop anytime you wanted to. So let's see you do it."

"I'm trying — I'm testing it out. Some tests take time."

"This is not a test. And you've already had enough time."

"Stop arguing with me and do what I say."

I had no choice but to get the fliers. When I got back Mom was complaining to Charlotte on the phone. I tried to write in my notebook but Mom kept interrupting to tell me what Charlotte said: "You should never do such things to your mother. You should be grateful to have such a wonderful mother."

After Charlotte, Mom called her sister and the women in her car-pool.

My notebook entry was: "Monday. The reward fliers saved my mother from buying cigarettes. She called everyone we know to tell them what happened and what she thinks about me."

15
That's My Mom

"Mom yelled all last night," I said. "Except for when she emptied the trash. And she did that about five times. This morning she yelled at me seven times, at Dad four times, and she threatened to give Emma away twice."

"I bet she's smoking," said Wendy.

"C'mon. She's gone over a hundred hours. I don't think she's smoking and neither does Dad. He said we have to hang tight, because this is the final cut for the big team."

"I'd read her journal."

"Wen-dy!" I thought about Mom while we waited for Dionna. She couldn't be smoking because she was so irritable. She always said smoking soothed and relaxed her. Besides, she was still drinking a lot of orange juice.

Dionna ran up the street. "The man with the paper bag on his head is missing," she said. "I haven't seen him since Saturday. It isn't like him to disappear."

"Maybe he found a new place to get spare change," I said.

"I hope so." Dionna didn't sound convinced. She said she'd look for him in the afternoon while she helped collect blankets for the homeless shelter.

At school Ms. Metzner was glad to hear I was going to the NSSS meeting. During progress reports, Carley said she was studying sign language at the Center for Independent Living, but she was having trouble learning the sign alphabet. I felt better knowing I wasn't the only one having problems with my project. Tomorrow was my turn to tell the class about Mom.

Carley finished her report by showing us how to sign "Hi. My name is Carley. I'm your friend."

After school I walked with Dionna and Wendy to the bus stop. We decided to watch today's and tomorrow's show together tomorrow afternoon. Wendy went to collect signatures, Dionna went to start her VCR, and I left for my meeting. I took the F bus to MacArthur Avenue, then walked to a small office building. A pretty woman with red glasses and silver-gray hair showed me the room where the meeting would take place at three-thirty.

"Do many kids come?" I asked.

"A lot. You'd be surprised how many. Lots of parents smoke. You're not alone."

I pretended to read while people filed in. I recognized

Bob Gaspardone, a boy from the eighth grade. I wondered which of his parents smoked.

Pretty soon the seats were filled and people sat on the floor. The meeting started. The first person to speak was a high school girl who described getting her dad to stop smoking. She used to pour water on his cigarettes and throw them in the wastebasket. Then one day she smelled a horrendous odor and caught her dad drying out cigarettes in the toaster oven. Her advice was: "When you see a cigarette, rip, smash, and crush it."

I wrote her advice in my notebook.

After her a boy talked about getting his mother to quit. He used a squirt gun to put out her cigarettes. He even put an ad in his school newspaper asking for another mother. I wondered who would want to be my mother and didn't pay attention until the boy said, "My best advice is: Don't give up. Make the smoker give it up."

I wrote that in my notebook. Ms. Metzner was going to like today's entry.

Then someone from the NSSS board talked and explained what they do. He described their programs for children and parents, when they meet, and how they want you to get your parents to sign up for their meetings.

"That's the most effective way for them to stop," said the silver-haired woman.

I knew there was no way Mom was going to come to a meeting. She'd already tried a group last year, the American Emphysema Association. It was a failure. Everyone had had to do the same thing at the same time: change brands, cut down, stop. At the end Mom had lied and said she'd stopped smoking so that she'd get a diploma.

"Look, Rayne," she'd said. "I had to lie. It would have been humiliating not to get a diploma. Everyone else was getting one, and I sure knew that Karl Arnold hadn't quit and neither had Dorothy Anson. Besides, I spent thirty dollars for the program and there were no refunds."

I had wanted to tell on her. "How can you lie like that? I don't understand. You didn't quit and you shouldn't get a diploma." But Mom had said, "You have a lot to learn, Miss Unsympathetic. Can't you forgive someone? Lighten up. You take everything so seriously."

I didn't think I did, and anyhow, she hadn't stopped smoking the way she'd said she would. Dad said it was hard for Mom to stop. He used to argue with her, but after that happened he said she was on her own.

The kids who spoke were answering questions. I asked, "What should I do if I think my mom is lying about not smoking?" My heart beat faster and I was sweating. But everyone made me feel it was the most usual question in the world. The high school girl said, "All smokers lie. At least once. Don't call her on it. Let her think you believe her. Don't give up."

Other people suggested ways to check up on Mom. They repeated what Wendy suggested: smell her breath and clothes. I wanted to ask about Mom's journal, but I was afraid they'd suggest I read it.

The silver-haired woman announced that the Thursday of next week was their monthly smokeout. "That's a good day for your parents to stop smoking or to see what it's like not to smoke for a day."

I left with handouts and a plastic replica of a black lung.

Riding home on the bus, I thought about our projects. Dionna was sure to get an A. She always managed to, even when she wasn't trying. Helping the homeless was something everyone cared about. All Dionna had to do was help one person and she'd have made her mark on the world.

I wish I had thought about that. My project was too dependent on Mom. No matter what Ms. Metzner said, if Mom didn't quit, I would feel like a failure, and I bet I'd get a low grade, too.

I used to think I was an ordinary kid, but I seemed to be changing into a loser and I didn't know what to do about that. I stared out the window and noticed several people smoking. Didn't they know it was bad for their health? Was the world full of losers and I hadn't noticed until now?

One loser was my neighbor Mr. Kramer. He died last year, and everyone said, "What did he expect? He smoked three packs a day." When I told Mom, she got angry and said, "You don't know what it's like to quit."

What I did know was that I didn't want Mom to be a loser. What I didn't know was why she said some things. Like once, on the phone she said, "One is all I need. Just one. I could buy a pack and smoke only one, then throw the rest away. No one would know. I'd only have one and I could keep on going. It wouldn't be like I'd started smoking again."

I asked how she could believe that. She told me to mind my own business. Later she said I'd understand when I was older. I'm older now, but I still don't understand. I don't think I will. Ever.

I looked at my watch. It was almost five-thirty. Mom would be home by now. So would Dad.

I hate to catch Mom smoking. She acts so guilty. And it's worse when she tells incredible lies.

Up ahead was Jim's Drugs. I'd be home soon. The bus stopped for a red light, and I watched someone run out of Jim's holding a pack of cigarettes. She ripped open the pack, pulled out a cigarette, and lit it. She was blowing a perfect smoke ring into the air when the light changed, the bus surged forward, and I cried out, "That's my mom!"

16
Fatal Addiction

I pressed against the window and waved my arms. I was so angry I could have jumped off the bus. Mom saw me. She dropped the cigarette and ran to her car. She fumbled with the keys, put the car in reverse, and raced to the end of the parking lot. My bus pulled past her while she waited for a man to cross the intersection.

My mind was reeling, going in a thousand directions at once. I remembered the first time I tried to get Mom to stop. She was smoking and I yelled, "Help! Help! My mom's on fire!" She laughed, but later she got really angry when I did it in our church's parking lot.

On the bus, I couldn't help saying out loud, "I will never forget this. I will never forgive her."

The man next to me said, "So? You think you'll be perfect?"

"Yes."

"Ha!" he said.

I didn't speak another word to him.

By the time I got home Mom was already there. She said, "It wasn't my fault."

"Mom, you had a cigarette. You were smoking!"

"I had a hard day. At least fifty people came in with problems with their car registration. Some yelled at me because they didn't want to pay the fines. What could I do? I couldn't change the rules. I had such a grueling day I deserved a cigarette. How was I to know your bus was going to drive by?"

"Mom, you're kidding yourself. You said you were going to stop. You would have had five days. Five! But now you're back to point zero. Forget one cigarette. You can't have any. Not even a puff."

"Honestly, Rayne, I'm trying. Look, tonight I'll really stop. I'm going to start a new me. Wait and see."

"I don't know, Mom. I bet you've been smoking all along."

"No, I haven't."

"How do you expect me to believe you? I think I should change to another project. This one isn't working."

"You don't mean that."

Mom got very pale and had a look on her face I'd never seen. She looked as if she were scared or something.

"Rayne, don't give up on me now. Please, one more time. I'm going to quit."

"You're just saying that."

"No, I'm not. Honestly. You've made me want to quit."

I was about to say no, but Mom took out a note from her purse and read:

Hi Mom,
  Don't forget today's method for not smoking is
to play with typewriter gum. I got you purple gum
because purple is my favorite color and I want you to
think of me.

                            Your purple daughter,
                            Rayne

She put her hand on my face and said, "Please."

"Oh, Mom. Okay, but remember, this is your last chance."

"Thank you, Rayne."

I opened my backpack and handed her the black lung. "This is what your lungs will end up like if you don't stop smoking."

"This is terrible." Mom bent the soft, rubbery plastic back and forth.

Later Wendy called on the phone. "You're being taken for a ride. Join my project. You know she's never going to quit."

"I'm not going to give up on her now."

"You can change projects and still help her. If you

work with me on the Nuclear Free Zone, we can get time off from school to go to meetings and demonstrations."

"If you'd asked me an hour ago, I would have said yes, but it's too late now. I've made my choice."

17
Last Chance Provinzano

After dinner Dad had a long talk with me about Mom. "I'm glad you decided to give her one more chance."

"I hope I'm not making a mistake."

"I don't think so. Just remember, some games make coaches old. Try not to get too upset when she has a relapse. I worry when you two argue. You know she loves you very much."

"Then why doesn't she stop smoking?"

"Things aren't as easy as they seem sometimes. Not everyone makes the free throws. You wait until you're older." He hugged me. "You're doing a good job. She really does like the notes."

"What do you think about my getting a smoke detector and putting it in her car —"

"Never! You want to cause an accident?"

"Well, how about in the bathroom or the bedroom, where she might sneak a cigarette?"

"Let me think about it. In the meantime, do your homework."

I did my homework until Dionna called. "Wendy told me what happened," she said. "Join my project. I need help. Big help. G.T. is still missing, and my parents don't want me to hand out fliers alone."

"What about my mom?"

"You can still help her. Besides, Wendy's sure to change her mind again and then we could all work together. Please. We'd make a good team."

"No. I'm staying with Mom, but I'll help find G.T."

Dionna moaned.

"But if I do change, I'll change to your project. Okay?"

"Do I have a choice?" asked Dionna.

"No. What happened on the show?"

"Everything. Bob and Kate were surprised in the boathouse by Jeff. Remember Jeff? He's Kate's ex-husband, and he went to jail for selling drugs."

"Yeah. I remember him. He was mean."

"He's still mean. He's threatening to kill Bob because he thinks Bob turned him in to the police."

"Oh, no. Did Bob?"

"Rayne! No, he didn't."

"I can't remember all the details. What about Francesca?"

"Incredible. Just incredible."

"So tell me."

"I don't want to give it away."

"Dionna, you can't tell me it's incredible and then say nothing."

"Yes, I can. I'll give you a hint: she's still alive."

"Thanks." That Dionna. I wanted to run over to her house and get the tape. But I had to wait until tomorrow afternoon.

I went downstairs for a snack. Dad was in the driveway loading orange juice into the truck. Emma was with him. "I'm going to deliver to the hotel and the restaurants by the high school. I was going to take you, but now I have too many stops to make and I'll get back too late."

I waved as he took off. Emma sat next to him in the passenger seat, looking noble and alert. I once asked Dad how come he complained about Emma not behaving in the house but then he always wanted her along when he made deliveries. He said she didn't bark in the truck. And she was good company. That made me happy. It meant he really does like Emma.

I looked around for Mom but didn't see her. I called but there was no answer. The basement door was open. I headed down. She wasn't in the main room. There was a plate of orange slices on the Ping-Pong table. Dad's old parka was on the table, too. Mom must have been working her way through our winter clothes. I found her in the back room where we stored the Christmas ornaments. She jumped when I walked in.

"What are you doing here? I thought you were going to the hotel with Ed."

"No, he's doing other deliveries and he's not getting back until after my bedtime. What's the matter? You look funny."

"You . . . you startled me, that's all. I'm fine. Go back to your homework."

Mom looked pale. The windows were open.

"Phew," I said. "It smells in here."

"Probably something outside. Have an orange slice." She propelled me to the doorway.

I took a slice and headed upstairs. Halfway up I turned. Mom was backing up. Her hands were behind her and something gray was curling around her neck. I didn't want to believe my eyes, but I had to. "That's smoke behind you, Mom. You're smoking! How could you? After all you said this afternoon." I ran upstairs, yelling, "That's it. I warned you. I quit."

Mom threw the cigarette on the floor and stamped it out. She ran after me. "No, wait. Look, Rayne, it's not what you think. There's no more cigarettes."

"What is it, then? You promised. You said —"

"That was the last cigarette of my life. I'm starting right now. Look in my purse."

"I'm tired of looking in your purse. I'm tired of you telling me you just smoked the last cigarette of your life." I was tired of arguing with her, too. Why was she doing this to me? Why couldn't she be the mother I wanted?

Mom stood there with her purse open, promising me that tomorrow she was starting her life over, thanks to me. She went on and on. I wanted to change projects. But if I changed projects, I'd have to tell Ms. Metzner what had happened. I didn't want to tell her Mom lied. I didn't want to tell the class what Mom had done. Now I knew why Francesca ran away from Craig.

"Okay, Mom. Okay. You're still my project. But I mean it — this is your last chance."

How many more times would I say this?

18
Black Lung Mania

The next day I dreaded giving a progress report. I prayed that someone had a project in worse condition than mine. Dionna went first. She described the city's plans for housing the homeless. She told us the Homeless Hot Line number and what was needed at the shelters.

Marissa showed us the restored mountain lion. The thistles were gone but up close the fake fur looked fake and the lion smelled moldy. Still, from ten seats away the lion looked real. Marissa reported that the Mountain Lion Coalition needed help to win their case to ban mountain lion hunting. She asked everyone to write letters to the superior court judge.

Ms. Metzner told her and Dionna to leave their information and the lion on the project table in the back of the room.

Brian described the new library for the Senior Center. Over half of the money came from the sale of chocolate-covered cherries. He refused to give free samples, but said he'd sell boxes of the cherries right after school. He put a carton on the table. Then Seiji invited everyone to go to Sacramento for a nuclear disarmament demonstration. He said they needed volunteers to help with the bus trip. Wendy looked at me and mouthed "No way."

At last it was my turn. I told everyone about the NSSS meeting and showed them the black lung.

"Gross," said Brie.

"I'm never going to smoke," said Steve.

"Has your mother stopped?" asked Aaron.

"Sort of, um . . ." Sweat poured out of me.

"Has she smoked since she quit?" asked Morgan with a sneer.

I couldn't say anything. My throat felt paralyzed.

"Don't feel bad," said Carley. "You can't help that."

"Yeah," said John. "It's not your fault. Have her see a hypnotist. My aunt did, and she hasn't smoked since."

Olivia said, "My dad kept sneaking cigarettes until he went to Smokers Anonymous. They meet at the main library."

Benny added, "Hey! That's where my uncle goes. You should see all the gum he chews."

"Thanks," I said. I really meant it. I put the black lung

on the table and sat down to listen to Steve describe what it was like to be an attendant for someone in a wheel-chair. I felt a lot better than when I started. But I still wished Mom could quit for good.

When Steve finished, Ms. Metzner said, "Class, I'm proud of you. Your projects are coming along well, and more importantly you've all found something you care about, and I can see you're working hard. Now, I have a surprise for you. Our class has been invited to participate in the high school's Homecoming game parade. Someone told the planning committee about our Impact on the World projects." She looked at Wendy, who put her head down on her desk. Wendy's mother always did things like that.

"I know we can have a terrific entry," said Ms. Metzner. "Let's have some ideas."

"We could carry banners," said Marissa.

"With the names of our projects, like Aid to the Home-less," added Dionna.

"Good. Good." Ms. Metzner wrote their suggestion on the blackboard.

"We could hand out fliers," said Steve.

"And sell chocolates," said Brian.

"We could have an information table at half time," I said, "where we answer questions." I'd stay at the table because I didn't know what I could put on a banner. I couldn't say my mom had quit smoking. The most I could say was she was kicking the habit, sort of — at least in her own way. Maybe I could carry a large foot.

Ms. Metzner said, "These are great ideas. What else?"

"Can the Dance for Peace girls dance?" asked Shannon. "My ankle is supposed to be totally better by then."

"Absolutely," said Ms. Metzner. "Anyone who wants to can join them."

"I could sign the music," said Carley, moving her hands to sign what she said.

"Wonderful," said Ms. Metzner.

"Let's carry the mountain lion," said Aaron.

"You carry the mountain lion," said Seiji. "I want to carry the whale."

"Me, too," said Bob. "We have to have the whale."

"The whale's too big," said Chris. "We need a car."

"Yeah," said John. "Then we could race around the football field."

"We need a truck," said Olivia. "So we can have a float."

"Rayne's dad has a truck," said Wendy. Miss Big Mouth.

Everyone turned and looked at me.

"How big?" asked John.

"A box van," I said. "That's a medium-size van."

"We need a flatbed," said Morgan, looking disgusted.

"Wait," I said. This was a chance to make up for Mom's

smoking. "My dad might be able to borrow a flatbed."

Silence.

"That would be so terrific," said Marissa.

"Fat chance," said Morgan.

"If anyone can get us a truck, it's Rayne's dad," said Dionna. "He's great."

First there were whispers. Then everyone started yelling what they'd do if we had a float.

"I'll ride on the top of the cab," said Olivia.

"Forget you," said John. "Our whale is going on the cab."

"No, my mountain lion," yelled Aaron.

Ms. Metzner had to shout, "Quiet! Hold on! Rayne, we'll wait till you check with your father before we make any plans. We'll understand if it doesn't work out."

After school Ms. Metzner went into the hall to talk to another teacher. I packed up my books and was walking to the door when I heard, "Oh, no." "Yuck." "That's really gross."

I turned to see Morgan eating the black lung. He'd take a bite, wave it in the air, then say, "Yum. Yum, yum. Mmmmm." He smacked his lips and black, dark, gummy drool oozed out of his mouth.

I gagged as I ran toward him, yelling, "You give that back. It belongs to the NSSS."

"I hope it's poisonous," shouted Olivia.

"It's only plastic," said Steve.

"It looks real," said Carley.

"I'm going to be sick," said Aaron, running to the wastebasket with his hand over his mouth.

"Ha! Ha! Yum. Yum," said Morgan. The drool now covered his chin and was dripping onto his shirt.

I grabbed Morgan's arm but he pushed me down to the floor.

"Hey!" yelled Brian. "He's eating my chocolates."

I looked up and saw that Morgan was just waving the black lung. There were no bites in it, and I could smell chocolate. "Give me my black lung, you phony pain in the butt," I shouted.

"Only if you eat it." Morgan laughed and ran for the door.

"You ate my chocolates. You have to pay," whined Brian, stumbling after him.

Wendy got to the door before Morgan and chased him back toward me. Dionna dove at him and knocked him into the projects table. John grabbed his legs. In the scuffle the mountain lion got knocked over and Aaron started screaming. Ms. Metzner came back in a flash and handed out detentions as if she were shooting a machine gun. I didn't get a detention because it was my black lung. But Dionna, John, Morgan, and the entire fourth row had to stay after school. Plus, Morgan had to buy a box of chocolates.

As I left Ms. Metzner said to Dionna, "What's happening to you? You've changed. First your marks and now this. You've always been such a good girl. What's going on?"

Dionna looked happy. I knew she was thinking that she was finally a regular kid — getting detentions and lectures. She had changed. So had Wendy — actually doing things without her mom and dad. What about me?

19
Down and Out in Corte Madera

Since Dionna had detention, she gave me the tape of yesterday's episode of "Corte Madera." Wendy left to collect signatures with her grandmother and I went home alone to record today's show. I also had to figure out how to persuade Dad to get a flatbed truck.

I wrapped myself in Aunt Margaret's afghan and nestled in my chair. For starters, I'd show Dad I was helpful at home. I grabbed a dirty sock Emma had wedged in my chair. I put it and all my dirty clothes into the laundry basket. I cleaned off the bureau and kicked my shoes into the closet.

I jumped back in the chair and wrote down a plan: find out about hypnotists and Smokers Anonymous, get homework done, take Emma for a run, and start dinner.

Smokers Anonymous met three nights and Saturday mornings at the main library. I looked for a hypnotist and was surprised: there were forty-one in the yellow pages and four in the newspaper. One man advertised himself as "certified and guaranteed." Another ad said, "One visit is all you'll need." One hypnotist offered a free telephone consultation.

In between homework assignments I watched some of the show. Francesca was in serious trouble. Wendy was going to be furious. She hated to admit it, but she really liked Francesca.

After I did my homework I practiced commands with Emma. I had her sit, which she did very well. I tried to make her stay, but she couldn't last ten seconds. The more I said "stay," the more excited she got. She rolled over and even tried to sit and lie down at the same time.

I gave up. "Want to run, girl? Huh? Huh?"

Emma raced to the door and barked. I held her mouth shut and said, "No bark," but she didn't understand. Emma would be a worse project than Mom. Emma got her leash and whimpered the whole time I changed into shorts and running shoes, even though I kept saying, "Don't worry, Emma doggie. I'm taking you."

I jogged until I came to Charlotte's street. She lived in a dark house behind a weeping eucalyptus tree. She worked at home, sewing clothes for people, and hardly ever went out.

Emma trotted up Charlotte's walk to sniff the door as I ran past the house. Charlotte didn't always answer when people rang her bell. I only visited if I'd called first.

Emma played with other dogs while I ran on the school track. I ran three miles before I went home. Dionna was already in the kitchen. "Detention was fun," she said. "I got to clean out Ms. Metzner's supply closet. My parents won't believe she keeps extra clothes, food, and a sample of *everything* she talks about." Dionna raised her eyebrows to say: "You know what I mean?"

I did, but then, I'd been having detentions for years. "What did you think of the magazines?" I asked. "Pretty hot, huh?"

"My fingers are still burning," she said. "But I'd need a week of detentions to read them all."

I rewound the tape of yesterday's and today's episodes. Dionna called the Homeless Hot Line to see if G.T. had shown up. And Wendy brought out juice and oatmeal cookies her grandmother had made us.

"No luck," said Dionna. "No one has seen him."

We fast-forwarded over the opening segment and commercials. "I'm timing this," said Dionna. "I bet it takes less than an hour and a half to watch two shows without commercials."

"It better," I said. "I have to be done by six or Mom will have a spasm."

"Better than a cigarette," said Wendy.

"Sometimes I wonder," I said. "She's so grumpy, Dad says she makes Billy Martin look like Mary Poppins."

"Hey!" said Wendy as we fast-forwarded over an ad

for milk. "What if you send G.T.'s picture to the milk company? They could put it on a milk carton with the question 'Have you seen me?' "

"That's just for kids," said Dionna. "Anyhow, I don't have a picture of him."

Tuesday's show started with two people in a lab searching through test results. "Who are they?" I asked.

"Beats me," said Wendy, shrugging. We looked at Dionna.

"You guys." She sighed. "You should take notes. They're Daryl and Dawn. They're trying to steal the latest formula for waterproofing clothes. Remember? It's worth a fortune."

Wendy and I muttered, "Yeah." "Sure." "You bet."

We paid attention fast when Kate and Bob were surprised by Jeff.

"You were right," I said to Dionna. "This *is* incredible."

"Makes up for a lot of dead spots," said Wendy.

Jeff laughed and waved a sword in Bob's face. Kate moaned. But just when Jeff was about to stab Bob, Craig limped onto the screen with a large bandage on his head. He was in The Locker Room. Andrea and Carla were there, too. "It's my fault Francesca was kidnapped," he said. "I didn't know she wanted to ask me to the dance. I listened to the message too late. Poor kid. She was just too shy."

"Why haven't they asked for a ransom?" asked Carla.

"They're probably waiting to see what happens to the guard they ran over," said Andrea. "He's in critical condition. Relax, Craig. No news is good news."

Craig wasn't convinced. He shook his head, saying, "Why did I chase her?"

The show cut to Francesca, blindfolded and tied up in a car. She could hear the kidnappers talking but couldn't make out what they were saying.

The show returned to Andrea, who was now at home talking on the phone. "It was a nightmare, Martin. That poor girl. And that poor guy Craig . . . Yes, Bruce and I are through. I'm moving. I don't know where . . . Thanks, Martin, but your girlfriend wouldn't understand if I stayed with you . . . I feel so dumb. Why didn't I notice his insensitivity earlier?"

"Yeah, why?" I asked.

"Fast-forward," yelled Wendy, "to the good stuff."

"No," said Dionna. "It's important to watch things as they happen."

At least she let us skip commercials.

Wendy and I groaned our way through Bob and Daryl and Dawn and Kate. After commercials, the show came back to Andrea trying on a dress at the mall.

"Guess Andrea decided the best thing to do was to go shopping," said Dionna. "My mother does that, too."

"Where's Francesca?" said Wendy.

Andrea walked by the girls who hung out at the mall.

"Look at their shoes," I said enviously. "Mine are disgusting next to theirs."

When Andrea stopped in front of The Locker Room, the show cut to Francesca. "Yay!" I yelled. "About time," shouted Wendy, tossing pillows. Emma woofed.

The car stopped in front of a warehouse. The kidnapper with long hair carried Francesca inside and up a long stairway. He put her on a bed, took off the blindfold, but left her hands tied in back of her. He looped a rope around her wrists and tied it to the bedpost.

"If you need me, just yell," he said, pinching her behind. "Ha! Ha!" He closed the blinds, pinched her again, then left.

She was in a tiny room. A scab-colored couch was next to the head of her bed. Across the room was a battered bureau with grease-stained rags on top of it. The camera closed in on Francesca's frightened face as the show ended.

"Wow," said Wendy, grabbing three cookies.

We fast-forwarded to today's show. After a brief glimpse of Francesca, Jeff pushed Bob into a pile of surfboards. As he locked the boathouse from the outside, he said to Kate, "No matter where you are, I'll be watching you."

"He is so sick," I said.

Daryl searched a closet while Dawn looked behind a blackboard. They were so boring that I decided the next time I taped a show, I'd watch it with Wendy and we'd skip over everything but the hot stuff.

Dionna could tell I was annoyed. "I'm sorry," she said.

"It's okay." I went to the kitchen for more orange juice. When I came back Andrea was in The Locker Room saying to Craig, "I have to sit down. My feet hurt." She plopped in a chair so heavily that dust came out of the sides. "I looked at seven apartments today and they were all terrible."

"Let me show you something comfortable," said Craig.

Andrea started crying as she tried on a pair of turquoise Reeboks. Craig patted her foot. "Don't worry. Things will turn out. I have a break due. Let's go somewhere to talk."

At a café Craig got a caffè latte and Andrea ordered orange juice.

"Dad will like that," I said.

"You were brave to get the license number yesterday."

"That was the least I could do," said Andrea.

"Someone had to do something," I said. "You were unconscious."

"I thought about you all last night," said Craig. "You're beautiful."

They sat for a long time looking at each other.

"I don't like this," said Wendy. "I don't like this one bit. What about Francesca?"

"She should have asked him to the Homecoming dance instead of buying her dad bowling socks," said Dionna.

I would have thought Dionna would be more sympathetic. Still, I agreed totally with her.

Andrea told her story and cried again. Craig put his arm around her shoulders. They planned to have dinner after she met with her parents.

"That's it," said Wendy. "That's just too much. He has his nerve. You know what's the matter with the people on this show? They don't have enough to do. Look at them. Now if they were involved in my project and had to collect signatures, deliver fliers, and make telephone calls, they wouldn't have time to be crying and putting their arms around each other."

Dionna and I were surprised by Wendy's outrage.

"I mean it. Francesca's kidnapped and tied up, and he's coming on to this babe."

"It's only a story," I said.

"You're jealous of Andrea," said Dionna.

"No, I'm not — what about Francesca?"

Francesca appeared again. The kidnapper untied her so she could eat and go to the bathroom. She stared in the mirror and asked, "What am I going to do? How am I going to get out of here?"

"Pray," I said.

"Visualize," said Wendy.

"Think," said Dionna.

Francesca grabbed her gray jacket from the back of the door and pulled a set of keys out of a pocket. The kidnapper had missed the small jackknife on her key chain. She hid it under the couch.

Back at the mall, police interviewed Mrs. Wallenberg. "What a shame," she said. "All that sweet little girl wanted to do was invite Craig to her Homecoming dance."

At dinner Andrea told Craig that her parents refused to see each other. "They'll talk to me and they'll communicate through their lawyers, but they are determined to go their own ways. The trouble is that the longer they stay with the new people they've met, the harder it will be to get back together."

"What more can you do?" asked Craig.

"I could hire a mediator and . . . and . . ." She started to cry. Craig put his arm around her again.

"I've thought things over," he said. "I know this is sudden, but if you don't have anyplace to go, you can stay at my apartment. I share it with my cousin. He's a wine distributor and travels up and down the coast. He's gone on a month sales trip."

"I don't know what to say," said Andrea.

Craig covered her hand with his. "Say you'll move in. I'll help you do whatever you decide about your parents."

"You're so kind," she said. "I don't deserve this."

"You're so right," said Wendy. "You are *so* right."

20
Thanks, but No Thanks

Dionna and Wendy helped me make string beans and baked potatoes for dinner. I let them taste the vinaigrette for the beans.

"Do you think your dad can get us a truck?" asked Dionna.

"I don't know," I said, scrubbing a potato. "I have to convince him I'm pulling my weight."

"What makes you think you're not?" asked Dionna, rinsing the beans.

"Mom hasn't quit. And if Dad gets a truck, what will I put on my banner? What will I say to people?"

"That's the biggie right there," said Dionna.

"Yeah," said Wendy, turning on the oven. "Your dad's fine. It's you."

"ME?"

"Look, you can't take it personally that your mother hasn't quit," said Wendy.

"That's easy for you to say. She's my mother."

"I mean, it's not like you failed or anything. *She didn't quit*," said Wendy.

"Okay, okay. But what will I do? Make a banner that says 'Mom didn't quit' or 'Mom's going to quit tomorrow'?"

"In a way she's like you," said Dionna, cutting the tops and bottoms off the string beans. "You know how you always say 'Just a sec'? Well, she always says 'I'm going to start a new me tomorrow.'"

"I thought you were my friend." I threw the potatoes in the oven, punched the timer buttons, and banged the steamer lid.

"Don't be so touchy," said Dionna.

"I still say you should get tough and read her journal," said Wendy.

"I can't. I told you, Mom and I have agreed that certain things are private."

"Okay, let *me* read her journal," said Wendy.

"No way."

"Why not?" said Dionna. "I'll read it, too. We'll be doing research for you. We'll only tell you if she's smoking. That way you won't be invading her privacy."

"What are you suggesting?" Were these really my friends? I had to be missing something.

"We're just suggesting something practical. We'll help

you keep your hands clean," said Dionna. "But it doesn't look like you want our help."

"Yeah, said Wendy. "Don't complain when you flunk social living."

They picked up their stuff and headed to the door.

"Wait," I said. "I . . . I . . ."

"Where is it?" said Wendy.

"In the third drawer on the right-hand side of her desk."

"RAYNE!" shouted Dionna and Wendy.

"I just wanted to be sure she was writing in it." I followed them to Mom's desk in the corner of the living room. Wendy opened the journal and Dionna leaned forward to see.

"Stop," I said, taking the journal back. "I can't let you."

They were disappointed but not angry. Wendy said, "You've changed. Last month you would have let us read it."

That night I told Mom about the hypnotists and Smokers Anonymous. "Forty-five hypnotists," I said. "Can you imagine? They're out there hypnotizing people like crazy, and you could be one of them."

"Thanks, Rayne," said Mom. "But I don't want to be hypnotized right now."

"Why not? Listen, you could see a habit-control specialist —"

"No."

"She's accredited. And you can call anytime, twenty-four hours a day. Or what about someone who does age regression and reincarnation?"

"I have enough troubles with my present life."

"Mom, look, here's an inner-quest awareness center. They specialize in goal achievement."

"I said no."

"What about the free telephone consultation?"

"Rayne, go away."

I wouldn't go away. I told her about Smokers Anonymous and suggested she go to a meeting. "There's one tonight at eight at the main library. You could make it."

That's when Mom blew her top and went ballistic. She yelled for twenty minutes. She brought up everything I had done wrong for the past three years, including "You never eat enough vegetables" and "Your table manners are a disgrace." She worked her way through the whole house: my unsorted junk in the basement, my things left around the kitchen and living room, and my disgustingly messy room upstairs. She criticized my dirty shoes and ended with a blast at my grades: "They're pathetic."

"My grades are *your* fault."

"What?"

"I've lost millions of brain cells from breathing your secondhand smoke."

Mom gasped.

"And I'm going to call a hypnotist if you don't."

"Don't you dare," said Mom. "What's happened to you? You used to stop bothering me when I told you to go away. But now you're like a pit bull: you don't let go until you've shaken me crazy." She slumped on the couch and stared at the floor.

Dad came to the doorway and motioned for me to come with him. "Rayne, we can't go on like this. Lighten up on your mother, and if you can't do that, then get another project. She's trying."

I told him I didn't want another project.

He talked for five minutes about what Mom had done for me, then said, "In our family we care about each other. Everyone would like to run down the court and make a lay-up, but in our family we pass the ball and set each other up. Got it?"

"Yes, Dad."

"Isn't there anything else you can work on for your project?"

I told him about the parade.

"Wonderful. Concentrate on that for a while. Can I help with anything?"

"It would be great if we could have a flatbed for a float. Do you know anyone who could lend us one? I sort of told the class I'd ask you."

"Sort of?"

"Well, actually, really."

"Do you want me to get a truck or not?"

"Yes . . . but there's a big problem: I don't know what I'll do for an entry if Mom doesn't quit. I don't want people laughing at me or anything."

"I can't help you with that. You've got to make up your own mind. What's it going to be: what you worry about or what you care about?"

"When you put it that way, it's easier to decide," I said. "I want the float."

"You sure?"

"Yes. Besides, it's time for me to pass the ball and screen some other players."

"That's my girl." Dad hugged me and went out to his office to make some calls. He came back in twenty minutes and said, "You've got a truck."

"You're not kidding, are you?"

"No, Pumpkin. You've got a truck. You can even have oranges to help decorate."

"No thanks. We already have a whale and a mountain lion."

"Tell Ms. Metzner I'll be the driver and I'll talk with her later about details."

I hugged him and said, "You're the best dad in the whole world."

And he is.

21
Rayne, Rayne, Go Away

Everyone cheered when I said we had a flatbed for the float. Ms. Metzner gave us class time to plan the design. The main argument was what to put on top of the cab. Brian surprised everyone when he suggested a six-foot chocolate-covered cherry that the candy company would pick up and deliver.

"No way," said Morgan.

"You've got to be kidding," said Brie.

Some kids made comments I can't repeat. Dionna rolled her eyes to the ceiling and Wendy mouthed "Why?"

"Put your candy on the flatbed," said Seiji.

"We need the whale on top," said Bob.

Olivia and Carley jumped in with their ideas and everyone began arguing.

Ms. Metzner said, "Hold it up, right now. Let's vote on this. I'll write down nominations. And you can have fifteen minutes to discuss them."

The nominations for the top of the cab were: the whale, the mountain lion, a missile, and the six-foot chocolate-covered cherry. The discussion got pretty heated and Aaron even screamed. At the end we voted. The results were: nineteen for the whale, six for the cherry, three for the mountain lion, and two for the missile.

Everyone was happy except Brie, Aaron, and Marissa, who kept asking, "Where should we put the lion?" So we voted to use the chocolate-covered cherry as a mountain and put the lion on top.

I wrote the dimensions of the truck on the blackboard. Seiji and Carley made a scale drawing, and Ms. Metzner marked off sections for different projects. The cherry was going to go in the middle of the flatbed, surrounded with fake palm trees from the Tiki Tiki Bar and Grill, where Marissa's father worked.

Olivia and Maya got half the area in back of the cherry to decorate as a child care center. Jason, Morgan, and Dionna got the other half for an Aid to the Homeless entry. Ms. Metzner told Olivia and Maya they could not use young children to make their entry look realistic. She also rejected Morgan's request to invite homeless people. Dionna looked at me and rolled her eyes to tell me what she thought of Morgan.

Ms. Metzner scheduled after-school meetings so we could work together on our projects or entries on the float. Since Dionna was going to the homeless center, Wendy and I decided to stay for today's meeting and work on our banners. Dionna said, "I'll tape the show and we can watch it tomorrow."

"Okay," said Wendy. "I liked watching two shows at once."

That was fine with me, too. The only problem I had was how to make things fine with Mom.

By the time I got home she was already there. I practiced the piano. I cleared my stuff out of the back hall. I even cleaned the bathroom, but she didn't appreciate anything. She growled every time she saw me.

The next morning her personality really crumbled. She woke up yelling, "Rayne, I told you to take the clothes out of the dryer."

"Just a sec."

"That's all I hear: 'Just a sec.' If you want me to stop smoking, you've got to help."

"But I *am* helping," I said. "And you haven't smoked for almost three days."

"Rayne cares what happens to you," said Dad.

"Yeah, I want you to get to five days," I said. "Ten — a hundred, even."

"Look, you two," said Mom. "I want —"

"You want a lot of things lately, Honey. Stopping smoking is getting to you."

"No, it's not," shouted Mom. "I'll tell you what's getting to me: your tomato juice and Rayne's following me around all the time. And —"

Dad, Emma, and I cleared out fast. We hid in the kitchen.

I asked Dad, "Is Mom really my mother — my biological mother?"

"What?"

"You didn't adopt me or anything?"

"No way." He hugged me. "Laura's really your mother and she's really your biological mother. She's just irritable from trying to stop smoking, and she's probably going to be very irritable for a long time."

"But all she does is argue," I said.

"All adults have to argue. If they don't, they're not being honest. Let's just say your mother is being hyper-honest right now."

"How come you're not like that?"

"Watch out. Last night I found out my best worker is leaving. I have to find someone fast before the holidays. It's not going to be easy. I may become pretty hyper myself."

Mom dragged the bathroom scale into the kitchen and said, "I hope you're happy. I've gained ten pounds."

I didn't dare say anything. Dad said, "You look good to me."

"How can you say that? I'm huge. If I gain another five pounds, I'm going to start smoking again." She stomped off.

I went to school wondering if Mom could get any worse.

Wendy and Dionna said she could.

22
Certified and Guaranteed

On Friday Mom tore up her Stop Smoking chart. After school I went to help Wendy collect signatures. Dionna joined us later at Wendy's house with a tape of yesterday's and today's shows.

Francesca was tied up again. She hadn't used the knife because the kidnapper kept returning. Bob and Kate were trying to get out of the boathouse. And Craig's toothache was worse. The best part was a huge fight between Bruce and Andrea. Bruce threw stuff around the apartment. At the end of the tape Andrea moved into Craig's apartment, which made Wendy furious.

"What about Francesca?" she yelled.

"What about Kate and Bob?" shouted Dionna.

"Enough about them!" I said. "I have bigger problems. This is day three and I'm afraid Mom's going to smoke. She's drinking so much orange juice I can smell her coming a room away."

"Follow her," said Dionna.

"That makes her mad," I said.

"Don't let her see you," said Wendy. "You've seen how Jeff operates."

So Saturday I hid in the bushes like Jeff and spied on our house. Mom spent most of the time washing clothes, talking to Dad, and cleaning out the basement. A few times she went to the side of the house, wearing Dad's old ski parka. Once she came back with flowers. Another time she filled a box with oranges from the bin inside the garage and carried it down to the basement.

After six hours I'd had enough watching. I went to help Wendy collect signatures. On the way home we passed a video rental store. Wendy pulled my arm and pointed to the tapes displayed in the window. There between *How to Repair Rattan* and *How to Tap-Dance* was *How to Stop Smoking*.

"That's a perfect idea. Mom and I could become friends watching it. We could be a team again." I rented the tape.

I waited until Mom was eating dinner before I told her about it. She wasn't enthusiastic, but she agreed to watch with me.

Dad wished me luck: "I hope it's a home run."

The tape started with Larry and Willow. "We're your non-smoking buddies," said Larry. "We want to help you stay stopped. So whenever you feel like smoking, just turn us on."

"Oh, Larry," said Willow.

"Oh, Rayne," said Mom.

I had a horrible feeling my homer was going to be caught at the fence.

"I like you," said Willow, looking sincere as the camera closed in on her face. "I want to know you. Tell me your secrets. I can help you."

"There's no way I'll tell this woman anything," said Mom. "In fact, I'm leaving."

"Wait, Mom. I'll fast-forward to another spot."

Mom smelled strongly of oranges. "You sure you're not drinking too much orange juice?" I asked. "Ms. Metzner said too much of anything can be toxic."

"You worry about yourself," she said, sitting back down.

Larry appeared in tights, breathing loudly and holding a six-foot cigarette. "See this?" he said. "It used to be my friend. But not anymore." He threw the cigarette on the ground and kicked and mashed it until he was sweating and breathing harder.

"That felt good. Didn't it?" he asked.

"Goodbye," Mom said. "I'm taking Emma for a walk."

"Can I go with you?"

"No, I want to be alone."

She left me sitting there, watching Larry and Willow run on a beach. When Larry lifted Willow onto his shoulders I turned off the tape and went to bed.

Sunday morning Mom was up before me. By eight o'clock she smelled like an orange.

I left to help Dionna serve breakfast at the homeless center. When I returned Dad's truck was gone. I figured he and Mom were food shopping. I started my homework and was on the fourth math problem when the basement door slammed. I looked outside and saw Mom hunched over, wearing Dad's old ski parka again. The hood was pulled over her head and snapped under her chin.

Then the nightmare happened: she lifted a cigarette to her mouth and smoked. I raised my hand to pound on the window. But what was the use? She wasn't going to stop. Ever. I should have listened to Wendy.

I returned to my homework. I couldn't concentrate. I ran downstairs and hid in the basement until Mom came in. She unsnapped the hood, washed her hands and face, then rubbed her face with a piece of orange. After that, she chewed one piece of orange and squeezed another into a cup. She dipped her fingers in the juice and ran them through her hair. When she started to rub juice on her sweater I yelled, "MOM! Give it up. I know your secret."

She jumped almost a foot.

"You said you'd quit."

"I tried."

"You lied. This is it. *I quit!* You're not my project anymore." I ran upstairs. Mom ran after me. "I'll get an F on my project."

"You care more about your project than me."

"All you care about are your cigarettes."

I locked myself in my room. Mom stayed outside my door and pleaded for an hour. She promised to see a hypnotist and called the one that was certified and guaranteed. She made an appointment for Monday afternoon. So I gave her another chance. No one would understand why. I wasn't sure I understood why myself.

23
What Did He Do?

After school on Monday Wendy, Dionna, and I went to my house to watch "Corte Madera." Francesca was agonizingly sawing through the rope on her wrists.

"I bet she rescues herself," said Dionna, giving Emma a piece of cookie. "She symbolizes the new woman."

"Are you kidding?" I said.

"Take it easy," said Wendy. "She's trying."

The show cut to Andrea unpacking her things in Craig's apartment. Craig had left flowers and a note.

"This is the first time I've seen her look happy," I said.

Francesca reappeared, pleading with the kidnapper to let her go. He kept saying no and laughing.

We went up to my room after the show. Dionna said, "I'd feel better if someone had seen G.T."

"Could he be at another center?" I asked.

"No. The hot line keeps a list of all the places offering shelter and I've checked them all."

I put Dionna in my chair and wrapped the afghan around her. "For good luck," I said.

Wendy said, "I have to distribute fliers on my way home. I'll ask about G.T. in the Senior Center and the library."

I was glad Wendy said that.

"How's your grandmother doing?" I asked.

"Great," Wendy said. "She even collects signatures while I'm at school. Don't tell anyone, but she doesn't like to be involved in my parents' projects."

When they left Dionna said, "Call and tell me how your mom makes out at the hypnotist's."

"If it works, I'll send my mom," said Wendy.

At six-fifteen Mom burst in the door. "The hypnotist was incredible, truly incredible. He looked deep into my eyes and said I was one of the most receptive subjects he'd ever had. In case you're wondering, retarded people and very analytical people make poor subjects."

"Nice to know you're not retarded," said Dad with a smile.

"Did he hypnotize you?" I asked.

"No. We talked about it, so that when I go tomorrow I'll be relaxed. Don't worry, I won't be put into a deep sleep. And he can't make me do anything I don't want to do."

"That's a relief," said Dad. "You're bad enough when you're conscious."

Mom glared, then said, "He kept telling me to relax my toes and breathe deeply. Every time he said to relax my toes, I did feel more relaxed. And by the time we were done, I felt peaceful."

I wanted to feel peaceful, too.

During dinner Mom said, "I have to make signs and post them around the house."

I helped. The first sign said:

SMOKING IS A SELFISH HABIT.
I DON'T WANT TO SMOKE ANYMORE.

"Put one on the refrigerator door," said Mom. "I don't want to gain any more weight."

Mom made a list of five reasons why smoking was bad for her health and another five reasons why she wanted to quit. She wrote:

WHY SMOKING IS BAD FOR MY HEALTH

1. Ruins my lungs.
2. Makes my heart work harder.
3. Causes cancer.
4. Makes me cough.
5. Hurts my eyes.

WHY I WANT TO QUIT

1. To live longer.
2. To breath deeply without coughing.
3. Not to have to buy cigarettes anymore.
4. To feel better.
5. To stop poisoning people around me.

I wished she'd said something about me, but I guess I was covered by number five.

Dionna called. "I found G.T. He was over by the Safeway. Wendy and I went there on our way home. I told him we'd searched everywhere for him. He said he'd used up his number of nights at the shelters and had to sleep somewhere else. It's too cold to sleep in the park, so he walks all night and sleeps in the library during the day."

"That's tough. What's he going to do next?"

"Get a job."

"What about the paper bag on his head?"

"If he works hard, I don't think it will matter. Do you think we can find him a job?"

"My dad needs someone to unload oranges. I'll ask."

I went out to the garage and told Dad about G.T. At first Dad got excited and kept asking, "He didn't offer you any candy, did he? Did he want you to go for a ride with him?"

"Dad, please. This guy hasn't even looked at me. He

doesn't have a car. And today was the first time he talked to Dionna."

Dad called Dionna. After what seemed like a hundred questions he said, "I'll talk to him, but I'm not making any promises."

24

Close Your Eyes on the X

For the first time in days, Mom got up in a good mood. She even made oatmeal for breakfast. "I'm ready for hypnosis," she said.

"Hmmm," said Dad. He kept reading the paper. Emma begged for a piece of toast.

"What are you doing after school?" asked Mom.

"I'm going to the NSSS to return the black lung."

"Thank goodness. It's not very nice."

I wanted to say something about her lungs, but I didn't. Dad nodded approvingly at me. I took Emma for a quick run before leaving for school.

During social living Steve said that Greg had a motorized wheelchair and wanted to be in the parade. Everyone wanted him to join us. Aaron asked, "Could he carry the mountain lion?"

We voted to have Greg and Steve lead the float.

At the NSSS I watched a film on cigarette advertising.

Mom's cigarettes had the best ad men. She smoked Mallarks, the cigarettes of kings. The ads didn't have real kings, but they did have lots of famous movie stars and even a few athletes. The bad thing was that most of them had died from cancer.

At the end of the meeting the pretty silver-haired woman reminded us that "Thursday is our monthly smokeout. Encourage your parents to stop smoking for the day. Tell them to listen to the public radio station. There'll be interviews with local groups that help people quit."

I left feeling recharged and committed to Mom. I took two copies of the radio programming and read them on the bus.

When I got home Dionna had dropped off the tape of today's show. I pulled the TV to the doorway of the dining room, so I could watch while I set the table. The show opened with Francesca cutting the rope. Then I did what I'd always wanted to do: I fast-forwarded over Francesca, past commercials, past Daryl and Dawn pulling up floor tiles, and even past Andrea dancing in Craig's apartment. I stopped only for the exciting parts, like Bob kicking open the door of the boathouse and Andrea nosying through Craig's desk.

A little later Dad came in and I told him about the NSSS meeting. We were talking about the smokeout when Mom burst into the kitchen, yelling, "I'M CURED!"

Dad and I hugged her. "How? What did he do?" I asked.

"We spent a long time on my last cigarette —"

"Wait a minute," I said. "You had a cigarette?" I was really angry. Dad put his hand on my arm.

"Yes, the last cigarette of my life. We talked about it — the heat in my mouth, the burning throat, the pain in my lungs. We talked about how it wasn't satisfying anymore. Then right in the middle of our talk I knew I'd quit. I was done, finished."

"How do you know it worked?" I was so disappointed that she'd had another cigarette I almost couldn't listen to her.

"I know. I just know. I want my body to live and enjoy life. Tobacco's poison. And so, folks, you're looking at an ex-smoker. All I have to do are these exercises to keep the energy currents flowing."

She handed me a list and called Charlotte on the phone. "I'm an ex-smoker," said Mom. Evidently, Charlotte believed her because Mom continued, "Yes, I'll show you how to hypnotize yourself, too."

I looked at the exercises:

Lie down.
Take a deep breath and hold it for five seconds.
Exhale slowly and mentally spell "relax."
Close eyes on the *x*.

I tried the exercises. When I closed my eyes on the *x,* I felt sleepy. I thought I was hypnotized until I stood up. Unfortunately, I was my regular self. When Mom got off the phone I helped her do them. She did seem hypnotized.

On the way home from school the next day Dionna said, "What do you mean 'seemed' hypnotized? Were her eyes glazed? Did she take shallow breaths?"

"Well, she wasn't her usual self," I said.

"I don't believe it," said Wendy. "Let me try the exercises."

"You're on," I said. "After the show."

Today's episode started with Francesca still cutting the rope.

"Ever notice how we're always waiting for her to do something?" asked Wendy. "First it was getting a job at the pet store. Then it was asking Craig to the dance. Now it's cutting the rope."

"You have to give her credit," said Dionna. "She goes on. She doesn't give up. You wait. She's going to escape."

"And take the kidnapper to the dance," I teased.

"At least *he* likes her," said Wendy.

The show cut to Andrea, sitting at Craig's desk.

"I don't know if I can take another day of her happiness," said Wendy. "If she starts to sing, I'm taking Emma for a walk."

Emma crawled out from under the couch, woofed, and ran for her leash.

"See what you've done," I said.

Wendy promised to take her for a walk after the show.

Andrea was looking through Craig's appointment book. "Look at this!" she screamed. Bruce's name was written next to the 2 P.M. entry. "I never told Craig Bruce's last name!" She called The Locker room, but Craig had already left. She dialed Bruce's office.

"You're too late," said Bruce. "I know you've moved in with Craig. You'll be sorry you left me."

He unplugged the phone and told the receptionist to go home for the day. Andrea called the police. The last shot was Bruce giving Craig gas, and lots of it.

While we walked Emma, Wendy told us that her group had collected over eleven thousand signatures.

"What about your parents?" asked Dionna.

"For once, and you won't believe this," said Wendy, "they aren't complaining. I worry that I'm dreaming and that I'll wake up in one of their enrichment programs."

After Emma's walk we tried Mom's self-hypnosis exercises. We did them standing up, sitting down, and lying on the floor. We did them with our eyes opened and closed. But nothing happened. Not even a touch of dizziness.

25
Smokeout Thursday

Mom left for work with the hypnosis exercises, the public radio schedule, and a twenty-four-ounce bottle of moisturizing lotion to use in case she got the urge to smoke.

"Good luck," said Dad.

"I'm rooting for you, Mom," I yelled.

When I left, Dad said, "Thanks for finding G.T. He's a good worker, but I'm amazed that he —"

"I told Dionna to make him take the paper bag off his head."

"I don't care about the paper bag. I'm amazed that he thinks about the whole business. He's given me some good suggestions for organizing deliveries. You tell Dionna she can be my personnel manager anytime."

I told Dionna at school, and she was happy to hear it. But Wendy grumbled, "Lucky you. You've made your mark on the world. Now you can kick back."

"He's only been working two days," said Dionna.

"Doesn't matter," said Wendy. "You're done and I'm not."

I was envious, too. Dionna always managed to come out on top. It was a good thing she was our friend. Otherwise, Wendy and I would have hated her.

Ms. Metzner read my notebook and talked to me privately. "You've done an excellent job, Rayne. Don't think I'm fooled by the comments in the notebook. I'm good at reading between the lines. I can tell your project has been tough."

I stared at her. How could she know so much?

"I'm always here if you want to talk about anything."

I sailed back to my seat.

After school Wendy had to go to the dentist.

"Don't let him give you gas," I said.

"Or tell you you have overbite," teased Dionna.

"Thanks a lot, you guys," said Wendy. "I hope there's a million commercials today."

Dionna and I went home to watch the show and record a copy for Wendy. The show opened with Bruce torturing Craig with a drill and a pick. Bruce scared me.

"It's a good thing Wendy didn't see this before she went to her dentist," said Dionna.

"I know. It makes me want to cancel my checkup."

Dionna left with the tape. "I'll drop it off at Wendy's," she said. "And you can count on me to help with your banner tomorrow."

I started my homework and turned on the radio to the smokeout station. A program about Smokers Anonymous had just started when Mom came home.

"I was listening to that program, too!" Mom sat next to me. For an hour we listened to six men and women tell how they stopped smoking.

One man had quit after smoking three packs a day for forty years. A woman had divorced her husband because she couldn't quit and he couldn't stand her smoking any longer. At the end of the program Mom said she was going to their meeting at the library tomorrow.

"Now don't get your hopes up," she said. "It's only a meeting. And I've only gone two days without smoking."

"Okay, Mom," I said. But my hopes were up.

After school on Friday Maya, Olivia, and Dionna helped me finish my banner. Red felt letters spelled MOM KICKED THE HABIT on a yellow satin background with purple fringe along the bottom. A blue felt foot kicked a white felt cigarette underneath the letters. I put a stick in the top fold so I could wave the banner myself. Ms. Metzner said it looked professionally designed and executed.

I rushed home to find out what had happened to Mom at Smokers Anonymous.

"It was so supportive," she said. "You talk only if you want to. You say, 'Hello, my name is Laura,' and everyone says, 'Hi, Laura,' 'Nice to see you, Laura,' 'Glad you came, Laura.' I felt so good being welcomed like that."

Dad and I smiled at each other while Mom continued: "I told them my story — you can talk as long as you want. No one interrupts. No one questions you. Other people talked besides me. They were all interesting. Everyone is at a different place. Some are trying to decide when to quit. They're still smoking."

"Not you, though," I said. "Remember that. You've already quit."

"Rayne, don't bug me. I'm doing my best."

I stopped talking right away. I wanted Mom to keep trying.

"Listen," she said. "At least I'm not sick. One woman has to have heart surgery, and she can't stop smoking."

"What's she going to do?" asked Dad.

"I'll find out tomorrow. I'm going to another meeting. I'm telling you, Rayne: I'm not so bad. Other people are in worse shape. You're lucky to have me for a mother."

26
Does She or Doesn't She?

Saturday morning, while Dionna, Wendy, and I watched a tape of Friday's show, Mom got four calls from members of her Smokers Anonymous group. She said, "They're checking in to see how I am. They offered to drive me to the meeting." She was happy. She was also nervous and irritable, but it was a relief to hear her laugh.

Dionna noticed a difference in Mom. "She's calmer."

"She's doing drugs," said Wendy.

"WEN-DY," I said, flipping Aunt Margaret's afghan around my neck and falling backward into my chair. "You're talking about my mom."

"What else is different?" asked Dionna.

"She doesn't disappear anymore. And I don't smell smoke on her clothes or in her hair."

"What about the oranges?" asked Wendy.

"No more oranges. I still worry about the parade. What if she came and smoked?"

"She's not going to smoke at the parade," said Wendy. "I trust her not to do that."

"I could be safe and change projects."

"That would be ridiculous," said Dionna. "You're almost to the end. Think of Francesca. Is she giving up?"

I scrunched down in my chair and said, "Maybe she should."

Later Mom told us about her meeting. "It wasn't like the other one. It was grim. The people were supportive and everything, but they ate candy and snacks and drank coffee the whole time. Hardly anyone sat still. It made me nervous. I wanted to get out of there fast."

"What about the woman who needs surgery?"

"She hasn't stopped smoking and she has to go to the hospital Monday." Mom smelled her jacket. "You know, for once I could smell whether people smoked or not. I never believed you could do that."

We went out to dinner for a reward. Mom warned us not to get too excited about her not smoking. "It's bad luck. Everyone in my group feels that way."

"We'll do whatever you want," I said.

"Don't be so wonderful either," she said.

That night I wrote in my notebook that Mom's attitude had changed.

All day Sunday Mom's group called to give her support. In between calls she ate. By midafternoon she'd had four Hershey bars, a Peppermint Patty, two bagels, and a thirty-two-ounce bottle of mango-raspberry soda. That was not counting breakfast and lunch.

"I can't go on like this," she said. "I'll be an elephant by Thanksgiving."

"Keep going," I said. "You can lose weight later. I'll help. I'll cook low-cal meals, I'll run with you, I'll —"

"I'm too heavy to walk back to the kitchen." Mom sagged onto the couch. "If I get a call, just bring the phone to me."

I brought her the newspaper.

"You'll be sorry when I'm the fattest mom at school."

"I'll love you no matter what."

"I have tomorrow morning off. I hope I stop eating by then."

"I'll stay home from school and help you."

"No, I can manage."

"Really, Mom. I could walk with you, I could do extra work in my math book."

"Go to school. I'll be okay."

I crossed my fingers. There were four days to the parade. She had to make it.

27
Some People Have All the Luck

At school Monday morning Aaron announced, "The Mountain Lion Coalition won their case! It was on the radio this morning. Hunting mountain lions is banned in California for the sixteenth year."

"Why him and not me?" said Wendy. "All I want is to make my mark on the world. I still have fifteen hundred signatures to go."

Dad and G.T. came by during social living. The kids were impressed by the size of the truck. Dad was impressed by the size of the papier-mâché whale. "That is really something," he said. But I was impressed that G.T. was wearing an Oakland A's baseball cap. When he waved at Dionna and said "Hi," Wendy and I almost fell over.

It took a half hour for Dad, G.T., and the whale boys

to secure the whale to the cab. The rest of us put things on the flatbed. We didn't have the chocolate-covered cherry, so we used a refrigerator box instead.

Dad said, "We have to be safe, so no moving once you're on the float." That meant Tamara and Shannon would dance alongside Steve and Greg in the wheelchair. Carley decided to walk with them because she moved a lot when she signed.

"We have a wonderful entry," said Ms. Metzner.

Dad agreed. He gave the class a ride on the flatbed so we'd know what to expect.

After school we set my VCR to record "Corte Madera." Then Dionna and I helped Wendy collect signatures at the Co-op supermarket. It was a discount day for members. By four-thirty we had one hundred and seven signatures.

We turned the petitions in and went home to watch the show. Daryl and Dawn had finally found WW2gX4, the secret formula for Water-Tex II, taped to the bottom drawer in the metal filing cabinet.

"That room looks worse than mine," said Wendy. "They pulled everything apart."

"Really," said Dionna. "That's serious trashing."

After Bob and Kate packed up their car, they took a walk on the beach. "It's so beautiful I could stay here forever," said Kate.

"You probably will," I added.

"Yeah," said Wendy. "With their luck Bruce will show up."

As if on cue, Bruce said, "You're too late. You'll be sorry you left me."

We fast-forwarded over three commercials to Francesca. A close-up showed the rope was almost severed. The kidnapper came in. He sat on the bed and caressed her neck. Francesca jerked away, dropping the knife behind the bed. It landed soundlessly on the shag rug.

"He better not hurt her," said Wendy.

The kidnapper kissed Francesca. She yelled. He laughed. Wendy and I threw our shoes into the hall and shouted, "Leave her alone!"

"Now what's going on in here?" asked Dad.

"Francesca's in deep trouble," I said.

The kidnapper tickled her. She kicked at him. "Don't go away," he said, closing the door. "Guess you won't 'cause you're all tied up. Ha, ha."

Francesca kicked again and slid sideways, falling over. She ended bottom up, wedged between the bed and the couch.

"That's one tricky lady," said Dad, laughing.

The kitchen door banged. Emma woofed and Dad swatted her. Mom saw Francesca upside down and kicking her legs. "What's she doing, advertising pantyhose?"

"She's kidnapped."

"Some people have all the luck."

"MOM!"

"If I were kidnapped, I could easily quit smoking."
Mom went back to the kitchen.

Andrea pushed her way through the crowd in front of
Bruce's office. She asked a policeman about Craig. "He's
on his way to the hospital," he said. "But don't worry,
he'll be okay. We're going to get that dentist, too."

Andrea sat down and moaned.

"Get up, girl. Get up," yelled Wendy.

"I'll help you," said Martin, putting his hand on Andrea's shoulder. "I know a short cut to the hospital." He
helped her into her car. "I'll drive. It's going to be rough.
We're going to take the old Frontage Road."

28
Countdown or Meltdown?

On Tuesday I made breakfast for Mom. I poured her a
glass of orange juice and said, "You've gone almost seven
days without smoking. I'm so proud of you."

Mom had dark circles under her eyes. "It feels like
seven years. It would be easier to die. What is this, French
toast? You trying to kill me off? Aren't I fat enough?"

"It's your favorite breakfast," I said.

"Oh, Lord." Mom put her head in her hands. She
barely ate anything.

Dad told me a woman in Mom's group had died, the
woman who needed heart surgery but couldn't stop
smoking.

At school Chris and Seiji showed everyone the morning newspaper's front-page headline: "U.S., Soviets OK
Missile Treaty." "It will be signed at the summit meeting," said Chris, passing copies of the newspaper around.

Brie brought in copies of the newspaper, too, so we could read the story about the mountain lion court decision.

"Darn," said Wendy. "If I'd gone on that bus trip, I'd have made my mark."

I knew how Wendy felt. Everyone was making progress or making a mark. But even though Wendy had only one more day to the petition-filing deadline, I was sure she'd get enough signatures. Then I'd be Rayne Provinzano, the big failure, the only one without a mark on the world.

I didn't cheer up until the NSSS meeting. A panel discussed how to help the ex-smoker through the holidays. I took information on massage, acupressure, and yoga. I even signed Mom up for a free swimming lesson.

Wendy and Dionna were waiting for me when I got home. The most boring part of the show was watching Andrea and Martin bounce along the old dirt road and skid in mud. Then Francesca, still on her head, twisted against the couch, landed on her side, and pulled the knife to her hand with her big toe.

"Way to go, girl," I said.

"I give her a 9.5," said Wendy.

"At least 9.75," I argued.

Bob and Kate were walking back to their car. There was a full moon and the roar of the ocean. They stopped to kiss.

After a hundred kisses and commercials, the show ended with Francesca cutting the rope.

"Not again," yelled Dionna. "Is that rope made out of nylon or what?"

"They should call this show 'Endless Rope,'" said Wendy.

"Really," I said.

Mom was in a worse mood for dinner. Despite five calls from her support group, two from Charlotte, and an offer by me and Dad to take her to the movies, she paced through the house complaining that life was too hard.

When I tried to tell her how great she was doing she said, "Success stinks."

"But, Mom, every day, every minute, and every second is a new record for you."

"Big deal. Each lousy moment of those records I want a cigarette."

The next morning Mom had new complaints. "Emma's driving me crazy. I could hear her scratch all night long. Somebody better do something or she's going away for the holidays."

I promised to give Emma a bath that night. In the afternoon Dionna and I were going to help Wendy collect signatures. I just hoped Mom didn't come up with anything else for me to do.

When I left for school she was on the phone, saying, "It's too hard . . . Okay, I'll stop for one minute at a time. But I don't see how that's supposed to work."

I worried about her all day. When I came home with

Dionna and Wendy, Mom was cheery. She smiled at us.

"Why are you so happy?" I asked, suspecting the worst.

"I made it to the living room without smoking," she said.

"She's clean," said Dionna. "I can tell."

Wendy nodded. "I think so, too."

I crossed my fingers. I was afraid to believe it.

The show opened with Bruce racing on the freeway, laughing uncontrollably. The police were hot behind.

"He's lost it," said Wendy.

"Really," said Dionna.

Andrea and Martin crossed the freeway just as police cars ran Bruce's car off the ramp below. "Maybe now he'll get help," she said. "I hope Craig's okay."

Martin yelled, "Let's go to the hospital." He gunned the engine and took off.

The kidnapper answered the phone. A voice said, "Kill her. The security guard died. She can identify us."

The kidnapper looked sad. He slowly filled a tray with a candle, a bottle of champagne, two chilled glasses, and a gun. He put on his jeans jacket and combed his hair.

Daryl and Dawn listened to footsteps in the hall. Carla showed off her new permanent. Andrea and Martin arrived at the hospital. Craig was unconscious, but then he opened his eyes and smiled at Andrea. At that moment she fainted. Craig called the nurse. Martin called her parents.

Wendy threw herself on the floor. "This show is exhausting."

Emma licked her face.

"Can I use the phone?" said Wendy. "I'm going to call the center to see if they've counted all the signatures yet."

A moment later everyone within a mile radius of our house heard Wendy scream. "We made it! We got enough signatures — more than enough. So if some don't qualify, we're still covered. We're going to have the Nuclear Free Zone on the June ballot. YAHOO!"

I hugged her and said, "That's great. You made your mark."

"I can't believe it," she yelled. "I made my mark. I made my mark." She danced around the room. Emma ran behind her. Mom brought in ice cream. "To celebrate your mark," she said.

Dad ran in, ready to swat Emma. When we told him what had happened, he threw the newspaper in the air and joined us for ice cream. Emma, too.

Later that night after I gave Emma a bath, I went to see if Mom needed any help. I couldn't find her. I looked everywhere, feeling sicker by the minute. She couldn't smoke now. She just couldn't. Dad came back from a delivery and said Mom was taking a walk. She'd be along in a minute. She had to think a few things over. When she finally got home I couldn't help myself: I smelled her breath and her hair.

"It's okay, Rayne," she said, patting my shoulder. "I didn't smoke."

From the sound of her voice I knew she was telling the truth.

29
Cherry Surprise

The day turned out sunny and bright for the parade. No fog. Just blue sky and millions of clouds.

Mom left first, saying, "I'll see you at the football field, Rayne. Emma, be a good girl and stay off the furniture."

I set the VCR to record the show and left next. "See you after school, Dad. Goodbye, Emma. Good doggie."

Dad waved and Emma woofed.

I met Wendy and Dionna at the corner. "I could hardly sleep last night," I told them.

"Relax, you've almost made it," said Dionna.

It was impossible to relax. Somehow I made it through the day.

When the last buzzer sounded, my class went outside to get ready. Eight parents came to help, not counting Dad and G.T. In twenty minutes the float was ready to go.

"It looks wonderful," said Ms. Metzner.

It really did. At first the chocolate-covered cherry

looked more like a volcano than a mountain. But after
we'd positioned palm trees around it and put the lion on
top, Wendy's mother said, "It looks real enough to be a
display at the natural history museum."

The parade started on time. Steve got to ride on the
back of Greg's motorized wheelchair. Greg carried Tamara's box and played the tapes. Tamara and Shannon
wore T-shirts with doves on them. They danced and took
turns carrying the Dance for Peace banner. Carley looked
as though she was dancing with them when she signed.

Ms. Metzner and our principal walked in back of the
wheelchair, carrying the school banner. Our float was
next. We were the fourth entry in the parade, after the
high school band, the table tennis club, and a rehabilitated
Ford pickup truck from the second-period car care class.

We rode through the main streets with people cheering
on the sidewalks. I waved to the crowd. Not everyone
was happy, though. Brie and Chris complained that we
were packed in too tight. Maya's father had spilled juice
on the lion, so the fur smelled more moldy than usual.
John and Matt said they were hungry. And everyone was
hot and seasick from the way the truck jiggled.

When we got back to the football field the mayor was
in the grandstand. Beside him were city council members
and the principal of the high school. Mom and Charlotte
were in the parents' section. So were Wendy's mother and
grandmother.

The road in the stadium had a lot of potholes. Dad maneuvered around them until he passed the bleachers and hit one. The truck lurched and pulled to the right. Dad hung on tight to the steering wheel and all of us stayed upright, but the swerving back and forth was too much for the whale. It pulled loose, slid down from the top of the cab, bounced off the hood, and sailed onto the field, knocking over our principal.

"Get it off! Get it off! It's squashing me," he shouted.

"Hold on. We're coming," yelled Dad. He and G.T. jumped out. They lifted the whale's head. Bob, John, and Seiji jumped down to help. Ms. Metzner and Carley lifted the whale's tail. The principal got up and G.T. helped him to the cab.

Ms. Metzner shouted to the rest of us, "Stay where you are. Don't move."

Those of us on the edge close to her couldn't move, but everyone else pushed to see what was happening. Brian tripped and fell into Morgan.

Morgan yelled, "Watch it," and shoved Brian.

Brian shouted, "You watch it," and pushed Morgan back.

Morgan yelled, "Watch this!" and kicked the cherry.

His foot went right through the molded plastic, making a gigantic cracking sound.

Kids yelled, "Wow." "Weird." "Gross!"

Red plastic foam nuggets gushed out of the cherry. They flowed over Morgan's leg, swamped the palm trees, and swirled over the side of the truck onto the field. Brian and Matt tried to stop the torrent by stuffing pillows from the child care center into the crack, but that only made the crack bigger and higher.

When the crack reached the top of the cherry, the side caved in and the lion crashed down. Infuriated, Brie and Aaron pushed Morgan off the flatbed into the whirlpool of red nuggets to avenge their lion.

"Stop! Stop!" yelled Ms. Metzner.

"Cut that out," yelled Dad.

I climbed on top of the cab and waved my banner. I pointed to Mom and shouted, "She hasn't smoked in eight and a half days."

The parade entries in front and back of us cheered. So did the crowd. The kids stopped fighting for a moment.

Mom looked surprised.

I yelled, "That's over two hundred hours without smoking."

The crowd cheered again. The coach sent half the football players to escort Mom down to the field. He sent the other half to stop the fight and fix the float. The tight ends tied the whale back on, propped up the lion, and stayed on the flatbed to keep everything together.

The mayor congratulated our class and told people

where our information table was. The principal said he couldn't wait to have us in the high school. The city council members said they expected us to make our city famous.

Ms. Metzner said, "Class, I'm so proud of you." No one mentioned the fight, and our float continued in the parade, with Mom next to me on the flatbed.

"You are really something," she said, hugging me. "I'm so glad you're my daughter. I don't want you to ever go away."

"Don't worry, I won't."

"I sure know that by now."

When we walked into the stands to watch the game she whispered, "We're not out of the woods yet."

"I know, Mom." I sighed. "But we're working together and that's what counts."

"You bet," said Mom.

After the game, Wendy and Dionna came back to my house to have pizza and watch "Corte Madera." Wendy's grandmother sent brownies and Dad made a salad with garbanzo beans and garlic croutons.

The show opened with Andrea sitting in a hospital bed. Her parents and Martin were on one side of the room. Craig was in a wheelchair on the other, holding Andrea's hand.

"Look, he's conscious," said Wendy.

"What about her parents?" asked Dionna.

"How's she going to decide between Martin and Craig?" I asked.

The show cut to Bob and Kate. Two men dressed as ninjas surprised them on the beach and tied them up.

"That is so like them," said Wendy. "Now they have another excuse to stay on the beach."

"I bet Jeff sent the ninjas," said Dionna.

We cheered when Francesca severed the last strands of rope to free herself. She hid in the living room while the kidnapper went upstairs with the tray. She pulled on her gray jacket with the red stripe on the cuffs, took the keys from the hall table, slipped out the front door, started the car, and was turning the corner before he discovered she was gone. She drove home on the freeway, laughing, her hair blowing in the wind.

"I don't want to be there when she finds out what Craig's up to," said Wendy.

"She's not home yet," said Dionna.

"You are so right," I said.

Mom scooped ice cream to have with the brownies. She said, "Let's take Emma for a walk before we go to bed tonight. I don't think I ever told you about the time I visited Aunt Irene and became the mascot for her cheer-leading team."

Dionna raised her eyebrows to say "O-kay!"

Wendy gave me a thumbs-up sign.

I was so happy I hugged Mom.

"The story's not that exciting, Rayne," said Mom.

Emma stretched out on the rug beside us. She'd eaten pizza crusts, garlic croutons, and even a brownie. She made satisfied moans in her sleep. I patted her and hoped her dreams would come true, too. When she snored I nudged her gently, saying, "Good Emma. Good girl. What a good doggie you are."